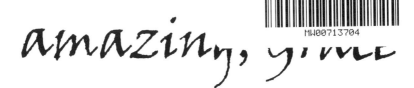

amazing, grace

Blessings
Jenn ! !

I miss you so
much !

All my
love

Roberta

ROBERTA GORE

eLectio Publishing

Little Elm, TX

www.eLectioPublishing.com

amazing, Grace
By Roberta Gore

Copyright 2015 by Roberta Gore
Cover Design by eLectio Publishing

ISBN-13: 978-1-63213-085-3
Published by eLectio Publishing, LLC
Little Elm, Texas
http://www.eLectioPublishing.com

Printed in the United States of America

The eLectio Publishing editing team is comprised of: Christine LePorte, Lori Draft, Sheldon James, and Jim Eccles.

To my mom, Audrey Rooney.

I miss you.

CONTENTS

*"Well darkness has a hunger that's insatiable, and lightness has a
call that's hard to hear . . ."*
~ Indigo Girls

Chapter 1
9/11/01

I wait behind my big sister Mary for my turn on the slide. Not the big one—
that's on the other side of the playground. There are lots of kids at the park
today. Everybody in our whole town got to play hooky. It's like a snow day,
except there's no snow. Mommy took us all home from school early—me and
my big sisters Mary and Bridget and my big brother Peter, plus our
neighbors Julie and Noah, and my baby brothers Shea and Sean. Noah and
my brothers are still in daycare, but Mommy grabbed them too. We could be
a parade, all us kids getting out of Mommy's big green van.

I was a brave girl this morning in my kindergarten class when Mommy
hugged me goodbye. She teaches art at Butler Elementary—that's my school,
and so she's just on the other side of the tunnel. I'm in kindergarten this year.
I know I'm being a big baby in the mornings when Mommy walks out the
red door that goes to the rest of the school, but I still cry like crazy. I can tell
Miss Dodge is tired of me. She takes these big gulps of air and kind of rolls
her eyes at her helper teacher. But today I pretended I had a button on my
lips, and I made my tears stay behind my eyeballs. And my friend . . . well,
she's my imaginary friend . . . held my hand. Her name—my friend's name—
is Clementine. I named her that because she smells like oranges and
sunshine.

"Gracie!" Mary says. I had climbed to the top of the slide, but forgot to
slide down. I'm a daydreamer. That's what Daddy says. The kids behind me
are yelling, so down the slide I go.

There's something wrong here today. The kids are okay—but the
mommies and daddies aren't. One mommy—she's sitting on the bench right
in front of my slide—is hiding her face, and her body is shaking up and

1

down. And there's a man sitting next to her. He has on an army outfit. He keeps trying to get her to lift up her face so she can see him. The man is like Clementine. I don't mean he *looks* like her. Clementine is a girl, like me, and this guy is a grown-up. But I can tell that the mommy can't see the guy. Like nobody can see Clementine. Except me.

I stand up and walk over to the lady. But before I can tell her that the man wants to talk to her, she gets up and walks away from him. I feel so sad for him because he doesn't even follow her—he just kind of folds himself up, like somebody on the playground without a single friend. The lady leans against a tree and hugs herself, like it's cold. And it's not cold today. It's bee-utiful. Really pretty!! The sky is blue blue blue and there's no clouds — not a single one. When I look back to the bench, the soldier man has already left. He's gone in a blink. Then some other lady comes running over and puts her arm around the cold lady, and I hear them talking about the Penna-gone. That's in Washington. Soldiers work there.

Mary, Bridget, and Julie run across the grass to the big-kid slide. Bridget and Julie are seven, and Mary is eight, so even though that other slide is *huge*, it's not too big for them. I'm only five. I watch the backs of my sisters' curly redheads vanish into the crowd.

I don't see Mommy. She was talking on her phone when we got here. Usually, she plays with us and swings the babies and stuff. Sometimes she goes on the monkey bars with Peter, but today she just sat on a bench and kept talking to her parents. They live on Long Island. That's in New York. I heard her telling them we got out of school early. I never see them, so I don't really feel like they're *grand*parents—more just Mommy's parents. She was whispering, like she didn't want us kids eavespeeking.

So I guess I'm the big kid in charge of the babies since everybody else is someplace else. I look over at the sandbox. My little brother Shea—he's a year younger than me—is slamming Sean and Noah with sand. I run over before Shea blinds one of the little guys.

"Stop it."

"We're just playing, Gracie."

"No, stop it. You're not allowed to throw sand."

Shea throws more before I can shake the sand out of his hand.

"Ahhhh!" cries Sean. Noah helps Sean wipe the sand away from his eyes while I yank Shea away from them.

"You're not the boss of me. Let go, Gracie. We're *playing*." Shea pushes me, and I fall down in the sandbox in between Sean and Noah. Then Shea tells us he's going to go play with the big kids.

"You guys want to go swing?" I ask.

"Okay," says Noah.

"Yeah, okay," says Sean.

I stand up, wipe the sand off my dress, take their hands in mine, and we head to the swings.

It's hard to lift the boys into the baby swings. They're not so little, and I'm not so big. I get behind Sean and wrap my arms around his tummy and try to raise him up into the swing like Mommy does, but he's too heavy for me, and we both fall down into the wood chips.

That's when I first see the man. He lives in my neighborhood. He has on a bright orange sweatshirt with a Baltimore Oriole on it. That's our baseball team.

***

Clementine sees Grace across the playground, and is careful to avoid being seen *by* Grace. Not twice in one day, anyway. This morning when she held hands with her, just to encourage her—just because the other kids laugh at Grace when she cries—Grace looked right at her, which gave the kids one more reason to laugh at the little girl. Anyway, she's trying to vanish as best she can.

Then she sees Bowen saunter across the grass, past monkey bars and seesaws, his hands in his pockets. He sprawls across a bench near the swings, lights a cigarette, throws one arm across the back of the bench. He has wavy brown hair with some gray strands mixed in, light blue eyes the color of the sky—today's blue sky—except she can't see his eyes today because he's wearing sunglasses, the *really* dark kind. But she's seen his eyes before.

"What do you want?" says a voice that isn't human.

Clementine gasps. She didn't see it slither over to her.

"Leave me alone," she says, wishing so much she could be one of those epic-type Guardians with an enormous sword and majestic wingspan. She glances at it—you're never supposed to look directly at them. This one has yellowish-orangey eyes, no eyelashes or eyebrows, and its skin reminds her of bark—old bark, old rotted bark. And it smells like sulfur and big black holes.

More of them surround her.

"You don't belong here," she says as she scans the playground and sees angels all over the place ignoring these demons who surround Clementine like they don't even care about them, like they don't even see them. Why are all these creatures right here, only bothering her? She knows it amuses them that they can rattle her. She wishes she could be less transparent. And then across the playground, she sees Bowen talking to Grace.

"You're with him," she says as she realizes why the playground is crawling with demons.

"Who are *you* guarding?" asks a creature to her left, this one seeming taller than the first, at least from what Clementine can see peripherally. She swings her head toward it quickly and takes in its greenish form, and then looks away fast. It almost blends in with the trees, except it's a more putrid, rancid-looking green. And it smells like death, and its eyes make her think of sewer grates.

"Isn't this the angel with the human name?" says one.

"The one who kissed the baby?" says another, and Clementine realizes they're distracting her on purpose—that Grace must be in trouble.

"And the girl named her. Like you would a dog."

She wrestles past them. One grabs her arm. Its claws cut her skin.

"Release me!" she says. And runs. Her arm burns.

Now Bowen's talking to Grace and laughing. He picks up her brother and holds him in one arm, and takes something out of his pocket. He starts to walk away and Grace follows, holding the other boy's hand, the boy with white hair like Clementine's. He's offering her brother candy. The boy takes it, laughing, and then Bowen sits down, placing Grace's brother on his lap. And Grace leaps onto the bench after them and pulls her brother with his bright red hair away from Bowen. She grabs the sticky candy out of his fingers and throws her whole body on the man, crying out for her mother—her mother who is sitting on the other side of the playground. The purple candy lies under the bench, covered in dirt. And Grace falls off the bench and onto the ground, grazing the wooden swing right above her eyebrow as she collapses.

"Mommmmmmmommmm!"

None of the humans pay any attention, not in time anyway.

And that's when the really bad thing happens, even worse than when Clementine kissed Grace five years ago and gave her this . . . *view* into the spirit world. Clementine stands stunned as she watches and, even worse, *hears* the sky rip apart. Then dozens of thirsty demons scoop Grace's spirit right out of her little girl body and go catapulting up and away from this playground, off this planet, far beyond the carnage left by terrorists on planes this morning.

Clementine releases her wings, six feet in either direction, blindingly white—not that any of these humans could see wings—except Grace . . . whose five-year-old body is currently convulsing on the grass. And she flies after the demons that took Grace's spirit into the hole in the sky.

***

I can't scream. I'm trying to, but my words are stuck inside me. I remember the wicked queen with the apple and how she makes Snow White eat it, and I know the purple candy is like the apple. The bad stuff the man put into the candy must have soaked inside my skin and poisoned my words. Even though I didn't eat any, it must be so bad, I'm dying anyway. I fall down, and my head hits something hard—the swing, I think. And now the man is looking at me. I can hear him talking to me with this soft, kind of whispery voice, like what a lizard would sound like if it had a voice, and he takes off his sunglasses and squats over me. And his eyes are like pools of water, and deep inside them I can see lots of smoke, like something's burning in there, like there's dead stuff under the water.

"Pretty girl, what's up?" He's laughing at me and smoking. He sucks on his cigarette for a long time, and then looks over at the boys. He wants to do bad things to them. I know it.

And somewhere high in the sky, way above my head, I hear the sky rip apart. I look up and it *is* ripping, fast, and there's a high screechy noise, like when my big brother Peter plays the violin, except this is a giant-sized violin, and the sound is filling the whole world.

And then everything goes black, and I'm flying right into that violin. I'm trying to scream for Mommy, but I can't hear myself. Or see. I'm wishing so much I could see when I feel my face and realize I have my eyes slammed shut.

So I open them, wide, but I still can't understand what I *do* see. All around me are big swirly clouds. It's like a sky-sized can of white paint, and somebody just poured in black paint, and now my body is the spoon.

I feel prickly sharp things underneath me, holding on to me. But I don't look down. No way. It smells like something died maybe, or worse. My throat hurts from trying to make words. I hear a loud motor sound, louder and louder.

And then the sharp things let go, and the bad smell fades away too. And it's bright. Somebody is carrying me, somebody strong. And it's really, really bright here—it's so shiny I have to squeeze my eyes shut again. Right before I do, I see bunches of white feathers.

And even though my eyes are closed, I know now that bunches of people are around me. I hear them. I hear a grown-up screaming "Call 911" and somebody else asking where the parent is.

"Gracie!" I hear Mommy's voice, and then I smell her and feel her, and I open my eyes.

"MMMMMMMM," I say, and I know *I'm* the motor. I want to tell her about the man who tried to steal Sean, and his voice, and the candy, and his eyes. I want to tell her I think I just flew out of the sky. Mommy is holding me and rocking me and telling me everything is okay. I can just make out the back of the man's orange sweatshirt. He's leaving. Fast. I want to tell her we have to catch him because if he doesn't get our little boys, he'll take somebody else's. He's got more poisoned candy in his pocket.

But I can't make words. Every time I try, all I hear is the motor.

***

"How could they do that? How could they . . . "

6

Clementine falls backward into seven or eight Guardians surrounding the humans.

"You can't split a living soul from her body! How . . ."

She hears herself. She knows she's losing it, losing whatever it is other angels have and she lacks.

"Kabshiel!" Guardians call her by her old name. Crying harder now, translucent tears streaming down her cheeks, Clementine moves away from them, closer to the humans.

"Is she epileptic?" a man asks Grace's mother.

A siren blares. By now the mother has Grace in her arms. They're rocking. Clementine remembers the day—almost five years ago—when the mother rocked her brand-new baby. The parents hadn't initially named her Grace; she was Siobhan. It was an exotic, beautiful Irish name for a stunning baby. Still in the hospital, Clementine saw her—this baby was her very first charge. And she loved her. The baby radiated light. Her spirit was pure. And Clementine knelt by the baby's precious head and kissed her on the forehead. She didn't know in that moment what she'd done. She didn't hear the chaos unfold.

Two men with a stretcher lift Grace.

"Kabshiel!" "Kabshiel!" Evangelos, a great big brave angel, sighs as he takes Clementine's shoulders and makes her face him. "All right. Will you answer me if I say Clementine?"

She looks at him. He's the opposite of Clementine. She's so thin she's almost translucent; he's totally solid, opaque. The white of his skin is like a prism; Clementine's is just a wisp of nothing. Evangelos must be a twentieth or maybe more generation Guardian. She's a first generation—totally inexperienced, an absolute travesty.

"You need to go with her. You. You are her Guardian." She tries to squirm loose, but he doesn't let go.

"I'm too small." She bows her head and hugs herself, allowing her wings to enclose her, hide her.

"You are her *only* Guardian. Be you small or huge, you're her promise."

"How did they *do* that?"

7

The angel shakes his head. He's not so sure, either. "I think it has to do with connecting."

"What? You mean, because she *sees* them?" So this *is* Clementine's fault. It's Clementine's fault Grace see the spirits.

"I think young children are generally protected. I think their innocence is a kind of . . . shield. They're less tempted, because they can't . . . imagine it."

Clementine feels herself shrinking. Maybe she'll get so tiny she'll disappear, and then Grace will be safe from her.

"Kabshiel," Evangelos says. But she won't answer to that name, ever. "Clementine." His voice sounds softer now, less judgmental. His tone compels her to look at him. "*You* rescued her. You flew into the battlefield *among them* and brought her back. Look at your wing."

She does. The edges of her right wing are shredded from all their claws. She raises her right arm to see it better. It hurts.

"A battle scar. You fought for her."

"And my name is my battle scar. She named me because she sees me. Because I kissed her. So . . . I'll never be Kabshiel again."

"So Clementine," Evangelos says. "Go."

They've closed the ambulance doors. The mother's friend collects the other children. Grace's mother will follow the ambulance to the hospital. But right now, Grace is alone. Inside the ambulance, she lies alone.

Clementine steps away from Evangelos and deposits herself inside the ambulance on the narrow cot beside Grace. She watches a man check her heart rate and blood pressure. Grace watches him too. The little girl's lips are pinched shut—her brown eyes huge as she studies all the machines. Clementine cuddles closer to her and whisper-sings in Grace's ear. The beeping of the heart monitor, racing moments before, slows down.

If these demons want a fight, Clementine thinks, she can fight. And so can Grace. But how can Grace be a normal child if she constantly talks to her invisible friend? The angel will have to hide from the little girl's sight, guarding her from hidden places. She kisses Grace's flushed cheek and whispers goodbye.

"One can never consent to creep when one feels an impulse to soar."
~ Helen Keller

Chapter 2
9/5/11

I'm in the woods.

I'm holding onto the branch above me as tight as I can—and trying hard not to let go. The bark is cutting into my palms, and I think maybe they're bleeding. My arms hurt, too, and my shoulder blades, and all the muscles in between. I'm trying to swing forward so I can rest my feet on the lower branch that's just a little bit in front of me. If I could just rest my weight on that branch and relieve the pain in my arms, then I could hang here longer until the shadow people below me find somebody else to bully. I call them that because they don't have bodies really, just a smoky form. I mean, I can't so much see *them* as much as I see where the space they inhabit is suffering from them being there. It's hard to put into words. It's like bone cancer, like what happened to Grandpa. He suffered because this tumor was ravaging his body. I couldn't actually see the tumor on the outside, but I *could* see the pain it caused. These shadow people look like fog, defined in space by seeping, infected sores.

The woods smell like wet pine needles and sulfur. The smell is making my throat hurt. It's not raining now, but I guess it did earlier. My hair feels wet, and my clothes are sticking to me. And I'm so cold.

I hear myself growl out loud, and then I'm scared they heard me. I make myself squeeze tighter with my fingers onto the branch above me, even though the sharp bark feels like razor blades on my palms. I keep squeezing until my feet can reach the lower branch. I swing forward again, and one bare foot kind of grazes it, and then I pull my other foot up and let the lower branch carry a little of my weight. I sigh as I relax my grasp of the prickly bark, but now I'm hanging on at a crazy angle, and by the time I realize I'm falling, it's too late to grab a tighter hold.

9

I fall smack into the shadows. I start to gag from the sulfur. But then I realize they left. I can hear them moaning or something, and now they sound like they're further away. I try to dig myself out of the leaves I fell into. I'm digging my way out when the wet leaves become a blanket, my knotted-up blanket, and the moaning is my alarm clock.

I had set my alarm—no, wait, three different ones—so I wouldn't oversleep. So my sisters wouldn't get in the bathroom first. So I could get a shower this morning. On the first day of school. On the first day of high school. Oh, God. *Oh*, God.

I keep one alarm clock on my night table. That one has a demure, tinkly sound, kind of like an old-fashioned telephone. I sit up in bed and see that one on the floor. Casualty number one.

Plus, I set a radio alarm way across the room. Yeah, that one's playing a Beatles song now, "While My Guitar Gently Weeps." I'll have to turn up the volume tonight for that one to help me at all.

And just to make sure I wouldn't oversleep, I borrowed this really aggravating alarm clock that kind of sounds like a tornado siren from my oldest brother, Peter. That's the one I'm hearing now. That's the one that must've blended in with my dream. It's still moaning, with background vocals by my sister Bridget fighting with Mary in the hallway downstairs. Then, it's *slam . . . click*. One sister has locked the other out of the bathroom. I missed my chance. So I get up, promptly smacking my toe on my little brother Sean's light saber.

"Ahhhhh," I moan.

"Grace, you'll have to skip the shower. Come and eat," Mom calls up to me from the second floor. We live in an old stone house, and even though it's not a big house, we do have three stories, not counting the basement. My sisters and I live in what used to be the attic. I love it up here. The slanted ceiling reminds me of a Hans Christian Anderson bedroom, plus it feels really private up here, which is nice with six kids.

"Gracie, I don't have room for you. You can take the bus," Peter yells up the stairs as he runs out the door.

I lean across my bed and turn on my Christmas lights. My lamp bulb blew a few months ago, and I kind of like these Christmas lights more. I have them strung all around my little third of our room, the room I share with my two sisters, Mary and Bridget. They have bunk beds on the other side of the room, and I have my little corner decorated in faded oranges and pinks and yellows, like sunset. Mom likes lots of color too. I think her secret mission is to expose us to every color God made, right here in our own little house.

I heave a sigh and massage my toe. I look across the room and study my new book bag, my semi-new lunchbox, and my favorite tee shirt I picked out for today. Do kids in high school carry lunchboxes? I don't care if everyone doesn't, but it would probably be tough if *no one* does. I like lunchboxes. I like my sandwich staying nice and cold, and I especially like everything not getting squished.

I hear Mom's voice from the kitchen, yelling up the stairs. "Get up Seamus! Sean! Now! If you *can't* get up, you can be rest assured that tonight you'll be going to bed at *seven.*" I listen to her get madder and louder.

Next I hear Bridget, incensed, screaming from the other direction.

"Dad, can you drive me? Peter left. I can't take the bus. I just spent an hour straightening my hair." My sister Bridget has really curly, really red hair. You can see that girl a mile out. I listen to her try to convince my father that it's to his advantage to be late for work so she looks her best on the first day of school. Dad works for an accounting firm in Baltimore, and the later he leaves, the more traffic he faces. But I can hear Bridget appealing her case, and she's usually pretty successful. Maybe she'll grow up to be a lawyer. I hear rain tapping on the roof. Be it car or school bus, Bridget's hair will be curly in minutes.

The bathroom door opens, and Mary joins the scream team. "I thought Tommy was picking you up."

"We had a fight," says Bridget as she passes Mary on the stairs up to our room.

Tommy's my sister Bridget's boyfriend. He graduated last year, but he's commuting to Towson University, so he's still pretty local, and he usually provides pretty efficient taxi service for my sister.

Mary enters our room, wrapped in a towel. "Gracie, get up! What're you doing? You're going to miss the bus!" She scolds me like she's my mother, which I think, secretly, she thinks she is. Both my sisters do, actually. Mary's the mother in charge of my being where I'm supposed to be—and not messing up once I get there. Bridget is more the mother who manages my

11

physical appearance—you know, what I'm wearing and whether or not it's cool enough. Generally, it's not. But they definitely trade off jobs a lot, and they both probably think they're each really more in charge than the other. Right now, Mary is staring at me with her mouth hanging open, and she's sticking her chin out in my direction like I'm a simpleton. "What are you doing?" she repeats.

"Waiting for the bathroom," I say as I sit up, trying to show her I'm awake and not the guilty party here.

The bathroom door slams. Now Bridget's back in there. She probably looked out the window and considered how quickly the rain would make her hair curl, so now I bet she's putting it up in a bun.

I lay back down, trying to imagine myself a high schooler. It's just so hard to see. I close my eyes and try to see the high school me, and instead I see a white-haired woman, wringing her hands with tears just floating down her cheeks. I've been seeing her a lot.

I can't tell if she's supposed to be some kind of future me, or maybe some crazy mishmash conglomeration of too many stories and movies, or just my twisted and overactive imagination. But I do see her—in my dreams when I'm sleeping and in my mind when I'm wide awake. Last week, I went to Cunningham Falls with Peter and the boys, and this young mother, barely older than my sister Mary, had lost her little girl. She was in hysterics, and all the lifeguards had all of us lined up and walking into the water. I was concentrating so hard, trying to look into the water—all murky and hard to see into—and all of a sudden, I saw the white-haired woman floating underneath the surface. I mean, just under the water. I screamed, and the people nearby thought I'd found the girl. Just then a security guard carried the little girl over the hill from the snack bar. She was fine. She had just wandered away for a snack. I didn't tell anybody what I saw. I kind of knew she wasn't really there, the white-haired lady I mean, because I recognized her from my dreams. Also there's something about her, about the way she looks, that seems kind of transparent. But I still felt so upset about it. I felt like, if she was going to present herself, especially when everybody was scared thinking a child had drowned, she should've had a purpose. But it turned out the girl wasn't in the water at all—so I felt like this white-haired lady was messing with me, or she was trying to tell me something, and I missed it. Or I'm crazy. And if I *am* crazy, that's something I think I'll keep to myself.

Then, just Saturday, my sister Bridget and I went to visit our great-granddad. He lives in an assisted living apartment, not far from our house. Papa Da—that's what all us kids call him—is a pistol. He emigrated from Ireland, the first in our family on my dad's side to come to America, and now that he's in his eighties, he's decided he's only going to speak Gaelic. I mean, exclusively. He's given up speaking English entirely.

Anyway, he'd fallen asleep, and Bridget had gone home, and I was just sitting in his room by myself. I was wide awake, and in absolutely sound mind and body. And all of a sudden, I felt this breeze. It was a pretty intense breeze, especially since I was sitting in a closed room with no windows. Then I saw this tiny little cloud kind of *wafting* across the room. I blinked to clear my vision. It was still there. I looked more carefully inside the cloud and saw bunches of people. There were these little people in the cloud, waving at me like crazy. No sound, though. It felt weird, but kind of nice at the same time. I think they were people I knew, or people Papa Da knew, but they were all people who had already died. I think I saw my Nonny and Uncle Charley. And there I sat, studying them, happy, and then—in the midst of all these semi-familiar people—there was that white-haired lady! What the heck was she doing on Papa Da's cloud? And she wasn't waving, either. She stood kind of apart, looking at me with this concerned look on her face, and then she started to cry. I wanted to talk to her and ask if she had some message or something for me, but as I was formulating words, the whole thing just vanished. I tried to blink and bring it back, but it was gone.

"Gracie!! Get out of bed now!! The bus will be here in ten minutes!" I leap up, catching a glimpse of my mother's vanishing figure in bathrobe and slippers.

"I'm up." I guess I nodded off. So I crawl across my bed, trip on the same darn toy, and throw it at the wall, which makes it make that funny *sizzle* sound, like when Anakin is having it out with one of the bad guys.

"Gracie, what are you doing? Are you *playing* up there?" Mom says.

"I'm up!" I call down the stairs, towel in hand. The bathroom, amazingly, is free. And before Cinderella's fairy godmother can say "Bippity boppity boo," I'm ready. I guess.

13

I study myself in the mirror we have hanging from our bedroom door. I'm wearing my vegetarian tee shirt that has a knife, fork, and spoon making a peace sign, with a caption underneath that says, "Eat in Peace." I've had it for a couple of years, and it's kind of faded now, and really soft from so many visits to the washing machine. It was huge when I got it, I guess, because it still fits. I love it. I guess I look okay. I have a sprinkling of freckles across the bridge of my nose that always look more prominent when I have a suntan—nowhere near as many as Mary and Bridget, but enough to give me the O'Shaunessy look. And my hair is kind of just hanging limply down my back. Rain is a funny thing. The same weather that makes everybody else in our family's hair get all crazy curly makes mine look like a box of sticks. Well, at least I look like myself.

I run down to the kitchen and wrestle my way into my rain slicker that probably just doesn't fit anymore.

"Gracie, where's your gym bag? Don't be late for cross-country practice," my sister Bridget says as she grabs her own bag. "We'll meet you in the locker room right after school." Bridget scrutinizes herself in the mirror. She applies lipstick. "And use your lock."

"Bridget, Tommy is here." Mom is looking out the window.

"Oh!" she says, pleased. And Bridget is gone. I guess Dad, or should I say, Mr. Chauffeur Man, is off the hook after all.

"You made up?" Mom asks nobody as Bridget slams the door behind her.

Mary looks at me and shrugs. Who needs soap operas when you've got Bridget and Tommy?

I think in my head how I don't want to run cross-country in high school. I don't say it out loud because that's non-negotiable in our family. My brother Peter is a freshman at St. Anthony's on a full scholarship for track. Mary and Bridget both run. Even my little brother Shea, who's only in eighth grade, trained with the cross-country team this summer, just to get a head start. My dad ran all through high school and college, and still does. And everybody thinks I have great potential. But I read in our school newsletter that Butler High School's Drama Club is doing *The Miracle Worker* this fall. I did a big report on Helen Keller in 6th grade, and I really love her. I think she's inspiring. I've kind of been practicing being deaf and blind in my room for the past two weeks. And I want to be an actress.

By now my brothers are in the kitchen, too, elbowing each other out of the way to get the last of the frozen chocolate chip waffles. The middle school bus arrives about five minutes after the high school bus, so this daily tornado hits hard, and then the dust settles fast. From 6:45 a.m. until 7:05 we're in chaos mode, every day from September 'til June. My mom teaches art at the elementary school about two miles from our house, and their school day doesn't start 'til nine. This is the first year, as long as I can remember, that Mom won't be taking at least one of us kids with her, now that Sean is in middle school. It's nice to imagine that now, once all of us have blown out the door, Mom will be able to settle down for another cup of coffee and a nice long bath. I pretend that, anyway. For Mom's sake.

I wait at the bus stop with Mary. She's on the outs with her clique of friends. I'm not crazy about a lot of her friends—when they hang out at our house, I overhear a lot of mean stuff. And I see them look at me, and then at each other, like something is hilarious. I just think they're, I don't know, not true friends. I've never been the most popular kid, and I'm kind of a nervous wreck generally—as a person—but my friends are true. So in that respect, I have more friends than Mary. I don't know what rule Mary broke in their little club, but currently they're kind of shunning her, so it's the big yellow cheese on the first day of school for Mary. I guess that's humiliating for a senior. As a freshman, I have no status. I'm just glad I'm not walking. It occurs to me that Mom's not running down the hill from our house to take our picture as we get on the bus for our first day. Mary would be mortified, but I wouldn't mind it. It's my first day of high school. It's a milestone.

"Just so you know, nobody carries a lunchbox in high school, Gracie."

I sigh. I think about saying, "Maybe someone will now," but my tongue might get stuck on the "M" sound. I mean, I stutter a lot less than I used to, but with the school bus looming over the hill, I'm pretty sure I'll stammer my way through my plucky comeback. I get on the bus after Mary, pretty sure she won't want to sit with me. And I glance at the bus driver first before turning to take in all the kids on the bus. Then, I look again. The white-haired woman of my dreams is my bus driver.

15

"Angels have no philosophy but love."
~ Terri Guillements

Chapter 3

The bus starts moving again before I sit down, and I almost fall into a couple of peoples' laps. Startled and maybe a little scared that she wouldn't wait for me to sit, I look at the bus driver again, who is also looking at me in the rearview mirror. She has long white hair like my lady, but that's where the similarity ends. Unlike *my* white-haired lady, who looks friendly, this one looks permanently ticked off. And currently, she's studying me like a hawk about to gobble up a mouse, a pitifully small mouse.

"Sit down!" she yells.

I feel like apologizing for getting on the bus. I realize the only free seat is the one next to Hayden Satalino. So I sit, fast, before she can bark at me again. Now I'm sitting next to the best-looking guy in my neighborhood, or at least he was in elementary school. He has curly brown hair, brown eyes, and he is *buff.* He's a chiseled kind of buff, not like a high school jock who'll grow up to be fat—more like a swimmer or runner kind of buff. Sadly for me, he's also probably one of the meanest guys. That's the scuttlebutt, anyway.

He used to "Ding-dong-ditch" us with his little gang of thug friends when I was in elementary school. I guess he was twelve or so then. My dad got really incensed. Every time there'd be a midnight knock on our door, Dad would leap out of bed and go racing out into the night, but he couldn't catch them. Then one night, and I remember us kids thought it was hilarious when Dad did this, he literally hid in the bushes next to our kitchen door and waited with his flashlight. Inevitably, a group of three or four boys came tiptoeing up the steps, whispering and giggling. We have this long stone path that winds all the way up our hill from the street, so Dad had lots of time to look forward to pouncing on them. He waited for one of the boys to open the screen and knock on the door. Then he leapt out from his hiding spot, screaming obscenities and flashing his light in their faces. He scared the heck out of them. He never told me what he said, verbatim anyway, but they never paid us a midnight visit again.

Hayden is very amused that I'm sitting next to him.

"Hey little G-g-gracie. Are you in high school now?"

I'm short, and so far, pretty undeveloped. I could pass for twelve, even though I'm fourteen. I'm pretty sure he's making fun of my stutter when he calls me G-g-gracie, which he has for years, along with lots of other kids. Terrific. What an uplifting bus buddy. I'm busy thinking about why Hayden isn't sitting in the back with his obnoxious friends when he tells me this is his assigned seat because the bus driver is racist.

"Huh?"

"Huh?" he repeats, kind of tilting his head and sticking his face right in mine.

A little part of me wants to ask him what he means, since he and our bus driver are both white. But mostly, I just want him to leave me alone.

I crane my neck to spy another empty seat. How ridiculous for a bus to be so overcrowded. Our stop is the absolute last stop on the route. And Hayden must own stock in Axe products because he reeks of it. I recognize the brand because my brother Peter likes it, but clearly not this much. I try burying my nose in my book bag.

"What are you, fourteen now, Gracie?"

I nod and take out my headphones. Maybe he'll leave me alone if I pretend I can't hear him. He says something sarcastic about my lunchbox, or maybe he just authentically likes Scooby Doo's Mystery Machine.

Eventually, we arrive, and I'm the first one standing.

Day One of freshman year isn't so bad. I'm not one of those kids who has lots of friends, but the ones I do have are true. Pearl and I met the very first day of kindergarten. She was the tallest girl, and I was the shortest in our whole class. My dad called us Mutt and Jeff. We met Morgan in second grade when she moved here from Kentucky. Morgan was really shy, and she still is. I remember her first day here. The teacher introduced her to our class, and Morgan started to cry, right there in front of a classroom full of kids. I got so embarrassed for her that I started crying too. As I remember it, I think Morgan was so confused that *I* was crying that she *stopped* crying. Anyway, at lunch that day, I went up to her and introduced myself and Pearl. The three of us have been best friends ever since.

I'm hoping I'll find at least one of them in lunch so we can sit together. I'm relieved when I see Pearl's blonde head above the crowd in the cafeteria—she's still tall.

I come from a family of curly-haired flaming redheads. My own hair is bone straight and this kind of muted copper color, at least when the sun shines. Inside, it just looks brown. Pearl has long blonde hair with just the right amount of curl. And she's one of those fourteen-year-old girls who really blossomed all of a sudden. She left eighth grade looking like she was thirteen, and she's starting ninth grade looking like she's a junior, maybe, or at least a sophomore. It's weird how that happens for some and not so much for others. I like to believe we'll all eventually catch up, meaning me and the other late bloomers.

Once we find each other, we scout around for Morgan, who's not as much of a midget as me, but not as easy to spot in a crowd as Pearl. I see her first, madly waving, and the three of us navigate the throng for a corner table. I'm so glad we found each other. I read a story over the summer about a girl who didn't have a single friend in lunch and wound up spending her lunchtime in the girls' bathroom. I've been imagining myself sitting criss-cross applesauce with my Scooby Doo lunchbox on the cold tile floor while the smokers puff away, stealing glances at the oddity who has joined their ranks. Anyway, that didn't happen. Pearl, Morgan, and I talk about our classes, and who's gotten cuter this summer, and who's in whose class. It's a nice break—something familiar in a sea of different.

When I get up to wait in the ice cream line, I hear a couple of "G-g-gracies." I look around to at least know who's saying it. When I was in fourth grade, things were the absolute worst. It's funny how grown-ups think middle school is the worst wasteland for kids. By middle school, I'd figured things out a little bit. Fourth and fifth grade—*they* were the worst years for me. My sisters had graduated to middle school. And Mary and Bridget were pretty popular, maybe not Queen Bee popular, but they were tall, athletic, sassy, and they have *always* been gorgeous. So they were good bodyguards when we were together in elementary school. But once I was on my own, kids bullied me a lot. And I couldn't fight back, not verbally anyway. I could've finger-spelled curse words, I guess, but who'd care?

I spy a couple of Hayden's ding-dong-ditch friends standing behind me in the ice cream line. They're probably the ones "G-g-gracie-ing" me. When I was on the bus once in fourth grade, the "G-g-gracies" got really bad, and Noah Dunne—that's my little brother Sean's best friend—went ballistic and starting hitting those guys over the head with his plastic Spiderman lunchbox. The bus driver turned the bus around, went back to school, and escorted Noah off the bus. I love that kid. I reserve judgment regarding the fact that neither Sean nor Shea had that kind of guts. I mean, I didn't, either. Anyway, today Noah's not here, so I just pretend I'm deaf as well as mute.

I like my classes, except for science. My conceptual physics teacher strikes me as a creeper. When he hands me the syllabus, he shocks me, literally, and for a millisecond, I feel like I'm going to throw up. But it passes. I get unexplainable bad vibes sometimes. If I bury them, they kind of fade away.

I go to cross-country practice after school and run really hard. I'm pretty fast, for a freshman anyway. I totally run on my toes. Before my family lived in Maryland, we lived on Long Island. Then my dad got transferred to Baltimore, and he packed us up, including my grandparents and great-grandfather, and moved us here. This was a long time ago. I was only two or three when we moved. The boys weren't even born yet. But still, I imagine myself learning how to walk on sand, so I'm a total toe-bouncer. I could be a successful burglar.

After practice, I cool down with Mary.

"So" she says, grinning at me and tilting her head in this devious, Mary-like way. "Do you like anyone?"

"Huh?" I say, eloquent as always.

"I mean, you know, a *boy*?" She raises her eyebrows and sticks her chin out.

I shake my head no, playing clueless . . . like I'd say if I did.

"What about Caleb? You know, that guy over there by the gate. I think he likes you. I saw him looking at you."

I shake my head again and feel the heat rising into my cheeks.

"I can introduce you to him, Gracie. Maybe if you tried to *look* like a girl, that would help."

I sigh. I steal a glance at him when Mary's not watching me. He *is* pretty cute. We walk past him and the rest of the boys' team on the way to the locker room. Once past, I fight the urge to turn around for one more glance.

Our team captain Becca has a car, a big old station wagon, and she drops my sisters and me home.

I decide to go visit Papa Da. I'm thinking he can help me figure out who this white-haired ghost lady is, or at least listen to me think about it. So I drop my stuff inside the door, grab my bike, and head off to Pleasant Living Senior Center. I love going places by myself. When you're one of six kids, you really covet alone time.

My Nana is there—she's my grandmother, Papa Da's daughter. She lives with us. Papa Da used to live with us too, but he started leaving burners on and calling dead relatives in Ireland in the middle of the night. A couple of years ago, he got dressed at two a.m. and went outside to wait for a bus. He thought he was going to Belfast. It was January, freezing, and we were all asleep. There he stood at the bottom of the hill, in his Sunday-best jacket and tie, eagerly waiting. We live in the woods, and there are no transit buses transporting anyone around here—day or night. When the newspaper guy delivered the morning paper, probably two or three hours later, there stood Papa Da, and by then he was delirious. He got hypothermia and had to be taken to the hospital. So now he's just a couple miles from us at Pleasant Living, and everybody's okay with it—except Papa Da, who protested the move by reverting, permanently, to Gaelic.

Nana is reading him the paper. When I walk in, she's reading about the most recent skirmishes in Iraq. This doesn't seem like such soothing material, but I think she feels like she's keeping his mind engaged.

"Gracie!" She's delighted I'm here. Nana is one of those people who makes you feel like your arrival just made her day. She's always telling me I'm hilarious, and gorgeous, and brilliant. When I spend enough time with her, I actually start thinking so too, at least until Mary and Bridget get their hands on me.

"How was your first day of high school?" she asks. "Da, today was Gracie's first day of high school. Can you believe it?"

"Gow much leh skayl neel bare-leh ug-um." At least that's what it sounds like to me. Nana and I look at him. I smile. She rolls her eyes.

"Nana," I say, deciding to give voice to a theory I have about White-hair. "I've never seen any pictures of your m-m-m-mom. I mean, why is that? Was she really young when she died?"

"My mother, Grace?"

"Yeah, Papa Da's wife. From Ireland. "

"She died before he emigrated, honey. My mother was his second wife, and she's a one hundred percent American mutt, like the rest of us." She cuts me a piece of pumpkin bread, or something that looks like it.

"Oh."

"You've seen pictures of my mother, honey. But I'll show them to you tonight if you're interested. Is this for a project, Gracie?"

I feel disappointed, unsettled. I was thinking my little white-haired imaginary friend was maybe some dead relative I didn't recognize. I mean, why else was she on Papa Da's cloud?

"No," I manage. "Do you know what Papa Da's first wife looked like?" Papa Da is really interested now. It strikes me funny that all the nurses at Pleasant Living think he's forgotten English.

"Hmm, tall, lots of curls, bright blue eyes. Black hair. She was a looker in her day, or so says your Papa Da."

"How did she die?"

"When your Uncle James was born. Childbirth. Why all the questions?"

I'm lost, thinking about my white-haired lady, who's small like me, with long, straight hair that kind of flows all the way down her back. If there's anyone in my family I could confide in, besides Papa Da, it's Nana. She wouldn't make fun of me if I told her I've been hallucinating. But I don't. I don't want her worrying that I'm a lunatic.

"No reason. Just curious." I give Papa Da a kiss before I go, and a big hug. He hugs me back. Sometimes when I hug him, I get these marvelous images of Ireland—the beauty and strength of it—and I get this painful sense of the loss he feels about his life now. I kiss Nana too and then head home. I do get lots of impressions from things when I touch them, but I can't read

22

them very well. Everything seems fractured, kind of the way things look when I open my eyes underwater and look up at the sky.

Talking about her was another dead end. If my white-haired lady isn't a dead relative with some message from the other side, what does she want? Why is she hanging around so much? And why do I feel like I almost remember her? I get back to our neighborhood pretty quickly. It's not even dark yet. Sean and Noah are having a light saber battle in Noah's backyard. They're in sixth grade now, and I think Sean knows he's got to put these antics behind him soon, but he's enjoying this last hurrah. They see me as I ride past.

"Hey, Gracie, Mom's mad. She didn't know where you went! Why didn't you answer your phone?"

My phone. I thought I had it on vibrate. I forgot at the end of the day to turn it on. Unlike the other O'Shaunessy girls, whose phones might as well be surgically inserted in their ears, I'm always forgetting to turn mine on. The vibration of my phone is the one "vibe" I'm constantly missing.

"How did you like day one of middle school?" I ask them, stopping my bike next to the huge weeping willow on Noah's lawn.

"Okay," Sean says.

"Okay," Noah says at practically the same second.

"I couldn't find our bus at first," says Noah. "Then I saw Shea. I couldn't remember the number or the bus driver."

"25," Sean says.

"Yeah, now I know, but . . ."

When they were younger—not so much younger, maybe last year—they used to take turns being Anakin Skywalker and Darth Maul. They'd battle all around the neighborhood. And they kept a soundtrack going. Neither one is such a terrific singer, and they'd be "dum dum dumming" at each other while they climbed trees and jumped over fences. Funny. Shea never got into all that. He's a different kind of kid. He's more grounded on planet Earth. But Sean and Noah—they're what you call kindred spirits.

I ride my bike across the street and prepare myself to face Mom.

"Millions of spiritual creatures walk the earth unseen, both when we wake and when we sleep."
~ *John Milton*, Paradise Lost

Chapter 4

I spend the rest of the first week of school going to classes and then, after school, cross-country practice. Thankfully, I only have to see my bus buddy Hayden in the mornings. When I get home, I do my homework. Pretty uneventful.

Secretly, though, I'm getting ready to audition for *The Miracle Worker*. Auditions are next week, and I checked the play out of the library on the first day of school. After I do my homework, or sometimes instead of, I hunker down with my Christmas lights and read. It's absolutely wonderful. I love how Helen can feel her way to words. Her sense of touch is her path to the world. I think about all the times I see things inside my head when I brush up against people, or when I touch something that belongs to someone—even something dumb like a pen, or even a coin, or a picture, or a doll, sometimes. It's something Helen and I have in common. Helen's more brazen than me, though. She's a lot more sure of herself and her place in the world. She wouldn't test everybody all the time and push the envelope if she was afraid to displease, the way I am. How would it feel to stop worrying, even for a little bit, about making everyone happy? And then, there's the whole talking thing. I'm like Helen in that way too. At some point, a long time ago, my mouth stopped working the way it's supposed to. Helen stopped talking because she had scarlet fever, and so she lost her hearing. I never lost my hearing. But I lost something. I just can't remember what, not during the day anyway. Sometimes, after I've been dreaming, when I first wake up, I think I do know why I stutter. I wake up to this ripping sound, and I know— somehow—that something inside me got ripped apart too. But the memories that come after the sound are hard to hold on to. I hold them in the palm of my hand, like a single snowflake, and watch them melt away. Maybe I'm afraid to know. Anyway, the more I read *The Miracle Worker*, the more I feel connected to Helen.

It's Thursday morning, and I'm getting on the bus, by myself this time. Peter has left for college, so that ride's out, but my sisters got a ride with Bridget's boyfriend Tommy. They said there was no room for me. I sit down in the empty seat next to Hayden, the only available one, as usual. I guess this is my regular seat now. He puts his arm on the back of my seat as I sit down. Yuck.

"Are you going to the Back to School Dance?" he asks.

"No," I say, madly searching for my earphones. He's got to be kidding. It's not that I don't see how cute Hayden is—but I hate it when he makes fun of me, and who wants to go out with a guy who tiptoes up to peoples' houses and wakes them up for kicks? Plus, it's almost like I can see the mean edge he hides behind, like some kind of outer layer. When my arm brushes his, when the bus makes sharp turns and stuff, I definitely feel darkness, and it scares me. It's like that feeling you get when you go down in the basement, and you know you heard something moving, but you're not sure what, and so you try not to panic because you hope you don't really have a reason to panic. That's how Hayden makes me feel, at least sometimes. I look past him to see my little brothers walking to the middle school bus stop.

Seamus, Sean, and Noah run around the climbing tree, playing some kind of game. Shea grabs a fallen branch and is staving them off like he's one of the Three Musketeers. A big part of me wants to leap off this bus and go back to middle school. It was less complicated. I'm just not ready for all this high school drama. I find my earphones, and I tune Hayden out. He takes his arm back.

At school, everybody's talking about the dance. And who already has a date. Pearl has a madcap crazy crush on a senior named Gavin something. We see him every day in lunch. She watches him until he looks anywhere near her. Then she goes all invisible. I guess he's okay, but not really my type. Morgan probably has crushes too, but she'd never say so. She's too shy. If a teacher ever asked her a question when we were in middle school, her ears would turn beat red. I remember last year in English, we acted out *Romeo and Juliet*. Morgan played the nurse in the scene with Lady Capulet when she's making all the bawdy jokes. Morgan's really smart, so she got all the jokes, unlike the majority of the class, and her neck, her ears, her whole face burned like a lobster. I got the job of prompter. I think my teacher was trying to spare me embarrassment because of my stutter. But the truth is, I would've loved to be one of the characters.

I guess I do have crushes of my own, I mean real-life ones, as in, not celebrities who I'll never actually meet, but I'm superstitious about speaking a crush out loud. So generally, I pretend I don't care. My sisters love to tell me I just haven't gone through puberty yet. Ha-ha.

After school, I almost go to the drama club meeting before cross-country practice. Auditions are next week, and I think it would be smart to at least get a script or hear the club advisor talk about what we'll have to do. I'm walking toward the auditorium when my phone vibrates in my pocket. I see it's from Mom, which doesn't make sense because she should be teaching first graders how to finger-paint about now.

"Mom?"

"Gracie, are you at practice yet?"

"I'm on my way. Is everything okay?"

"Sweetie ran away, and I've looked and . . ." Sweetie's our beagle. Mom sounds upset and out of breath. "I think I left the kitchen door open."

"Do you want me to come home?" I've stopped in the hall. I'm turning around now, heading back to my locker to get my stuff. "Mom?"

"Can you ask your coach?"

"Sure, I'm on my way. How come you're home? " I ask as I grab my book bag and lunch box and sprint down to the locker room.

"To check the stove. I started thinking I'd left it on, and I got worried. I kept imagining . . ."

"I'm on my way, Mom."

Once I read a story, or maybe it was a movie, but anyway, it was about this mother who imagined her children dying in the most absolutely horrendous ways, every time any of them left the house. I mean, she thought really awful things were happening—like gruesome car accidents and buildings blowing up and bloody crime scenes with everyone riddled with bullets. Nothing awful ever did happen to the kids in the story, but the mother never calmed down. Well, that's my mom.

I find my coach standing outside. She looks and sounds like a pixie—I mean, I almost imagine her to have little fairy wings, and she's barely older than Peter. I like her.

I get permission to leave, and so instead of running the course today, I run home. Part of me gets frustrated that Mom would never think to call any of the other kids to help her find the dog. Last time Sweetie ran away, the two of us walked for miles, and then the friendly neighborhood dog catcher called us—all this happening while the rest of the family was hunkered down in the family room watching a movie. If I didn't know better, I'd think the rest of the clan doesn't care about the dog. But my mom is a serious worrier. And even if I did have it in me to ignore her pleas for assistance, I can't imagine being able to enjoy whatever I was so busy doing, knowing she's walking around the neighborhood by herself. So I go.

I see her when I'm a couple of blocks from our house, with Sweetie's collar and a box of Milk Bones. The two of us canvas the neighborhood. We don't have a really organized way of searching. Every time we hear a dog barking, we just head in that direction.

"Sweetie!" Mom calls.

"Sweetie! Sweetie!" we call together.

"She always finds her way home. Right, Mom?"

"Right. Good day?"

I shrug.

Finally, arm in arm, we take a break and walk home. We're sitting on the back steps. I'm telling her about the dance, and about how I don't really want to go.

"So why should you, Gracie? You don't have to go. Better you have one less experience watching the way these kids bump and grind."

That makes me laugh. I agree with her and feel a little better, more relaxed. Every time a car drives by, we're up again, hoping someone's bringing Sweetie home. Finally, when it seems hopeless, along comes our neighbor, Mr. Bowen, holding Sweetie. We both leap up.

"Are you missing something?" he says as Mom takes Sweetie and puts the leash on her.

Mr. Bowen lives across the street, next door to Noah. He's one of those guys who always looks like he just heard something hilarious, but for whatever reason isn't supposed to look like he's amused. That, in turn, always makes me think he's smirking. I can't tell how old he is. He has barely any gray hair, but I think maybe he dyes it because he's kind of wrinkly. And he must work out because his body looks kind of young. I know it's sexist, but for some reasons *guys* who beautify themselves to look younger than they are seem creepier than women who do it. I don't like him. I can't really say why, exactly. It's not just the dyed hair, or the fact that I think his curly hair is a perm. There's just something about him. And his eyes are so blue he looks like an alien.

"Thank you so much," Mom says. "Where was she?"

Mr. Bowen shakes his head. "I have no idea. Up to no good, I guess. I just pulled in and there she was." Sweetie is now madly sniffing at his pant leg.

"I didn't think you had a dog," Mom says.

"I don't," he says and shrugs.

I hear canvas rip, and for a breath of a moment, I see Mr. Bowen in some other place, and a great big black dog—a lab, I think—is jumping up, resting its paws on his chest. Then the ripping noise stops, and I'm standing in my backyard next to my mom. I feel sweat tickling my backbone.

"Well, thank you so much, really." Mom looks at me, waiting for me to chime in.

But crazy glue just flew out of Mom's workroom window, squirted a line of itself across my lips, and even if cute guy Caleb was standing next to Mr. Bowen asking me to this big deal dance, I couldn't say a word.

So I smile and nod and keep my feet firmly planted next to my mother. As Mr. Bowen turns and walks down the hill, I watch him put his hand in his pocket, and for some loopy reason, I feel like he's carrying poisonous candy.

***

29

Clementine watches Bowen. She doesn't want him anywhere near Grace. His face, handsome on the outside, is a façade. Has always been. Even when his wife wept that she'd been wrong to speak against him, it was deception. She hadn't been wrong at all. Beyond his smile, Clementine sees his spirit, darkened by unchecked desire—and death.

She follows him to his house—only a house, not his home and wonders what he did to entice Grace's dog. She wonders what he wants now. Why did he do that?

"What I'm looking for is not out there, it is in me."
~ Helen Keller

Chapter 5

Audition Day. I'm perched on the edge of my bed, and I've laid outfits on the floor. I'm looking at three different looks for Helen. I had a lot of trouble figuring this out. Fashion isn't my strong suit—just ask my sisters. I know I want to look like Helen, but what would Helen be wearing if she was walking around Butler High School? I'm really hoping I'll get to do the dining room scene. I should consider underwear then. Helen crawls under and over the table in that scene, and Annie Sullivan drags her across the room at one point. So choice number one is a skort and a white blouse. But it's kind of a short skort, and I'm thinking maybe it makes me look more like someone auditioning to play field hockey. My lucky jeans and favorite tee shirt are choice number two, obviously not chosen because they make me look anything like Helen Keller, but because I just think I'll be less nervous in comfortable clothes. I already know I won't pick choice number three. My mom sewed me a milkmaid costume for the seventh-grade wax museum. Sadly, I'm currently the same size. That's probably the dress that looks the most like something a little girl in the 1800s would wear, which is why I pulled it out. I looked at a bunch of pictures of Helen Keller online, and there's one of her in a dress that looks exactly like my milkmaid outfit. But do people wear full-fledged costumes when they try out for plays?

"Grace! Ten minutes!!!" I grab the skort and jeans, and toss the milkmaid under my bed.

"Gym bag," Mary says as I walk into the kitchen, pointing back up the stairs, clearly exhausted by the burden of being my sister.

"I don't have gym," I say.

"Practice."

"Oh. Um, I'm going to try out for the play today."

I try to act like this isn't going to be a big deal to anyone and feign sudden interest in whatever yummy snack Mom has placed in my lunch box. And then Dad is studying me, all of a sudden tuned to Station O'Shaunessy, his paper kind of dangling into his coffee.

"What?" Dad says.

I put on my sweatshirt and shove my skort into my book bag, unmercifully wrinkling it.

"Gracie, you already made a commitment to cross-country. You can't just go do some other thing." I'd love to smile at my father, nod, and walk out the door, but if you knew John O'Shaunessy like I do, you'd know this is a man who requires a response.

"Well," I say, momentarily derailed. "I thought I could . . ."

"Your mother and I paid $300 for you girls to play a fall sport. You can sing with the choir next year."

I'm confused now, wondering what the heck he's talking about. What choir?

"No, Dad, it's not . . ."

"Bus!" says Mary.

Just like that, I'm free. I run out the door.

Naturally, both Mary and Bridget are riding the bus today. So once we're seated, they continue. Mary pokes her head between Julie Dunne and the girl she sits next to.

"Gracie, don't be insulted you're not running varsity on Saturday. Megan Bailey is a senior and Coach always runs the upper classmen on varsity at the first meet. But you're faster than her, Gracie. You'll get her spot next time."

I nod to Mary across the aisle as the bus barrels along. I'm not jealous of Megan. I'm glad she's getting to run varsity. I want to be Helen Keller.

We arrive, and I hustle off the bus before Bridget or Mary can say anything else. I head for class and peaceful anonymity.

Before I know it, I'm in my last class. And it's 2:15. I'm reading *Killer Angels*, or so my English teacher assumes. Really, I'm hiding behind my book imagining I'm Helen. I close my eyes and imagine I'm feeling for vibrations—on the table, on the floor—and I imagine myself smelling everything around me. I don't smell Mrs. Keller's perfume—that's Helen's mom—but I imagine it. The perfume, I mean—smelling lemony and warm, like sunshine. But now, all I smell is lye soap. I imagine Annie Sullivan would wash with it, so that'd be what Annie would smell like. I can smell lye soap, so I know Annie is in this room with me, but where's everybody else? I look for my mother. I imagine she has small, fragile features that Helen can touch. I'm alone in this room with Mrs. Lye Soap. I start touching the chairs. They're all empty. My heart starts beating hard. I run and smack my face into the door. My chin rams right into it. It burns, and tears well up. I find the knob on the door, and it won't turn. It's locked. I'm locked in with Annie Sullivan.

Brring.

Confused at first, I realize school's out. I pack up, aiming to avoid my teacher's glance, in case I was grunting or doing some other weird thing when I was lost in the dining room. But he's busy talking to someone about the Civil War, so I head out. I'm taking the side hall to the auditorium just on the off-chance my sisters are stalking me in the lobby.

I make a quick right, still more in Helen's dining room than a high school hallway.

"Where are you headed, Gracie?" I register that my sister Bridget is standing in front of me, blocking my path, and I feel incredible disappointment.

"Um, I'm trying out for the play."

"No, you're not." Bridget laughs as she redirects me to the stairs. "Gracie, you're not an actor. You can't even really speak in complete sentences. Come on. Let's go to practice."

Okay, let me explain something about myself. Truly, I'm not a wimp. I actually have lots of backbone. Last year in middle school, these boys were making fun of Stephen Phillipson. He's autistic, and if you trigger his rage, he'll put on a real show. I guess that's what they were working for—a show, with Stephen as the unsuspecting main attraction. I was sitting at the next table, and before I could stop myself, I was up and in this one boy's face, Connor Myers—who is a punk—and I punched him right in his pretty nose. Honestly, I was more surprised than Connor Myers was. I was suspended for three days.

33

But this . . . bravery . . . it needs a trigger. I remember looking at Stephen when Connor invited him to sit at their stupid table, and Stephen thought that meant Connor and his little posse actually wanted him to be their friend. And then Stephen understood what they actually wanted, and he got this look on his face—like total defeat, like he knew nobody was ever going to want to be his friend. His cheeks were all blotchy and red, and his eyes were welling up with tears, and for a second, I felt like I *was* Stephen, like we were both prisoners in this awful, lonely world. And that's what made me snap— that these boys were hurting us like this on purpose because they wanted a laugh.

And Bridget escorting me away from my dining room scene, like she's some kind of wise mother hen, makes me feel trapped, but it's not really triggering rage. So I go.

Practice is uneventful. I run hard. We're running the course today, 3.1 miles, and I'm fast. So fast I'm done long before Mary and Bridget come out from the woods. I wave to Coach. She thinks I'm going off to do my cool-down. Well, I'm going, all right. I run inside, sprint up the stairs, and hightail it to the auditorium. It's 4:30. All the posters say auditions run until 5. I can make it.

I step inside. People turn around and study me, not for long, but long enough to make me blush. A boy I've seen in the halls motions me over. He's sitting next to Ms. Dawson, the drama teacher.

"Are you auditioning?" he whispers to me.

I nod. He points to the stage. I see a pile of papers, walk up as quietly as I can, pick one up. I write that I'm auditioning for Helen. I'm not sure what to write regarding experience, so I leave it blank. I give the form to the boy and sit down. There are two girls on stage doing the dining room scene. The girl playing Helen makes no sound. I wonder how she can manage this scene without grunting or whimpering. And she has her eyes closed. That seems weird to me too. Why would Helen close her eyes? When Annie starts dragging Helen across the room to make her pick up the twentieth spoon Helen has thrown, the girl playing Helen madly exposes her butt to the audience. Some kids chuckle, and I remember my skort stuffed into my book bag, or even my lucky jeans. Here I sit in gym shorts and spandex. Not how I planned this. But it'll have to be okay. I pull my hair out of its ponytail, and try to smooth it down with my fingers.

"Grace O'Shaunessy?"

I turn around and see Ms. Dawson is looking at me. "Grace? Your turn. Everyone else has read, honey. Girls, is there someone who'd be willing to read Annie again?" Ten hands shoot up. "Lisa? Thank you. Go ahead, girls. There's no time to practice first. It's almost 5. This will be the last scene, ladies and gentlemen. I'll post the cast list on the website tonight."

I walk onstage with Lisa. I know she's a senior, pretty, one of those girls for whom everything she touches turns to gold. As I recall, my sister Mary doesn't like her. Lisa tries to get me to go back and get a script. But I already know this scene. There aren't any words—it's all stage directions. And how can I be reading stage directions when I'm Helen Keller?

And then the scene starts, and Grace kind of fades away. I'm Helen, and it's all about the vibrations I can't feel, and the smells not here in this locked room, and Annie's lye soap, and my shins hitting the table, and these darned spoons I don't want to hold. And I'm hungry, and I'm sad. And most of all, I want my mother back. "Mama!" I scream in my heart, but I don't have words yet, just feelings. My mouth is locked up. I madly brush my cheek to the world, my sign for mama, but she's nowhere. She's left me. Annie has sucked her up. I hate Annie. I don't understand these spoons, and I hate them too. I throw them, all of them, and I try and try to run away. I feel her grabbing at me, and dragging me, and I can't figure out how to get away. "Mama!" my heart screams again and again, but it doesn't come out. I'm just moaning something that sounds like a motor, and I'm crying, and tired. I feel a glass of water, so I pick it up and I drink a bit, and then spit it in the direction I think Annie is. Then *I'm* all wet, too, soaking wet. Annie threw the whole glass at me. My mouth is open, and I'm choking. Annie grabs my hand, and she bangs some kind of pattern into my hand. It's curious. I'm quiet as I feel this new sensation of her fingers in my hand. I wonder what it means.

Then, just like that, the scene is over. I'm Grace, all wet, and I don't know now if I was supposed to spit the water at Lisa. I steal a glance at her, and she looks upset. Okay. So maybe not. But it's in the script. No, wait a minute. I was supposed to spit *food* at Annie, and then *she* was supposed to throw water at *me*. Oh boy. Well, there wasn't any food. And the water was sitting on the table.

"What's your name?" Lisa says.

"Grace."

"I can't believe you spit at me," she says, for my ears only, looking pretty disgusted.

Ms. Dawson is standing on the floor below the stage, holding my form. "That was . ." she reads my name and looks up, "amazing, Grace. You're in ninth grade?"

I nod.

As I walk up the aisle, she asks me if I know the drama club's website address.

And there stand my sisters in the back of the auditorium. I walk to the back, expecting a lecture. Instead, Bridget says, once I'm close enough, "You don't know it, Gracie. Go find out what it is."

"Know what?"

"The website. Go! Before she leaves. So we can find out if you got Helen!" I stand for a moment, shocked. My sisters actually look proud.

"Everyone entrusted with a mission is an angel."
~ Moses Maimonides

Chapter 6

The ride home is quiet. I replay the audition in my mind, and the feeling I had when I was Helen and not Grace. The joy of it. The release. I rest my head on the back of my seat. We pull into the driveway and up our hill, and I'm confused by all the flashing red and blue strobe lights. Becca stops her car in front of our house.

"Wow, something must be going on across the street, you guys," she says.

We unfold ourselves and our book bags from Becca's backseat.

Mary and Bridget head for the house. I want to know what's happening, so I walk toward the action. It's getting to be twilight, and as I run down the hill and across the street, I recognize my brothers, mother, and most of the neighborhood. I listen for words—try to read faces. Was someone hurt? My brother Seamus sees me. He runs across our neighbor's lawn and meets me on the sidewalk.

"Noah got off the bus, but he never went home!" he says.

"Noah?"

"The cops are here because they think someone took him."

I feel uneasy—like someone's watching me. I scan the crowd. And then I see her—my white-haired lady friend. I blink a couple of times, look away, and look back. She's still there. She's not looking at me. She's listening to a police officer, who's talking to a small cluster of grownups. I leave Shea to listen too. As I get closer to her, she looks at me. She's been crying. She blinks, and tears swim down her cheeks.

"Find the boy," she whispers. And she's gone. I mean, literally. I mean, she evaporates, like a genie or something.

I look around Noah's backyard. Police lights are flickering. I hear a woman crying, hard, and more people are arriving. It's pretty dark by now.

People are arriving with flashlights, passing them around. I see Dad jogging across the grass to Mom. She has her arm wrapped around Sean's shoulder, and my parents look around. Then they see Shea and me. Dad walks over.

"Baby, go home with the boys and lock the door. Your mother and I are going to help search."

"Dad . . ."

"Go home."

"I can help too. I can search."

"Grace, you can help by going home with your brothers, locking the door, and staying put." His voice sounds really serious, and kind of strained, like a rubber band pulled as tight as it can go, right before it snaps.

When we get home, we lock the door, and Mary makes hot dogs and macaroni and cheese. It tastes like cardboard. All us kids eat in total silence. We watch the news. It's weird to see our neighborhood on TV. They flash up a picture of Noah. It's his fifth-grade yearbook picture. That's weird too. We have the exact same one on our refrigerator. Mom and Dad don't come home, and I guess everybody goes to sleep. I mean, we act like that's what we're doing. I try. But I feel like I'm supposed to be out there, finding Noah. I think about what it's like for people whose loved ones drown at sea. When they stand along the shoreline, waiting for some rescue boat to bring them back, they must want to dive in—even if it means they'll drown too. That's how I feel in my room, waiting.

I toss around in my bed for a while, looking out my window and seeing a light show of flashlights and red and blue police lights. I think about White-hair's words.

Find the boy.

She sounded like she thought I could. Or maybe I imagined it. Maybe it was the wind. I stare at the night sky and let the flashing lights blend with the moon. I remember Noah running up and down the aisle of the bus on his little six-year-old feet, smacking everybody with his lunchbox for me. That's when I really start crying. I smother the sound of it in my pillow and try to make myself stop. It takes a long time.

38

I'm flying. I fall out of the sky and through some hole into another place—some dark place of hollow-sounding laughter, the way it sounds when people laugh inside a cave. I've been here before. I hear the church hymn, "Amazing Grace." Someone is whistling it. And it's warped-sounding. Whoever's doing it is holding notes a long time, and they're all kind of sharp. It makes me scared. It makes me feel like, wherever I am, someone awful knows I'm here, and they're using the song to make fun of me because Grace is my name. Then I realize the reason it's dark is because I've closed my eyes. That's why I can't see anything. So I open them quickly, and all I can see, for really far on every side, is mist and a kind of steamy drizzle. I see all kinds of shadows. I can't tell if they're people or clouds, or even animals maybe. I'm not really falling anymore, I'm floating. I see what look like hooks or fingers or claws, and they're trying to touch me. The rain is soaking me, and then I'm caught and carried someplace else. I'm not sure if it's the air itself carrying me, or those fingers. The laughter is louder here. I think my tears are mixing with the drizzly rain, and I'm trying so hard to scream for Mom, but my mouth won't open. The M-m-m-m-m sound is stuck inside my head. There's a flash of white. I see wings, and then something is carrying me away. I hear distorted voices, and it sounds like a lot of people yelling in a cave, and someone screams, "Is she epileptic?" So I try to make myself be quiet, and the M-m-m-m-m morphs into my alarm clock.

I wake up. I had the creepy dream again, but it's already fading, and I let it. I lie still, watching it fade away on the horizon of my mind. Just as I sigh, relieved that it's gone, I remember Noah.

The house is quiet. I get up, tiptoe out of our bedroom, and go take a shower. Afterward, I go looking for Mom and Dad. I tap on their bedroom door and poke my head in. Nobody's there. I go downstairs. The kitchen's empty too. I never heard my parents come home, and now I'm worried something worse happened. A tingly feeling tiptoes up my spine. Still in my bathrobe, I step into our backyard. Both cars are here. I'm scanning the neighbors' yards, and see nothing—and then, for just a millisecond, I see something really weird. If I was a drug addict, like the kids who hang out under the footbridge, I'd think I was having some kind of LSD flashback, but I've never touched anything more potent than Tylenol. So as I'm scanning the yards, it's like all of a sudden, I see the trees and houses of our neighborhood like some big backdrop on a stage, and the backdrop literally *rips* in half. And even weirder, I *hear* it rip. And after it rips, there's another neighborhood behind it—ours, but different. And in this other neighborhood, it's yesterday, and I see my brothers' bus, and it stops, and I watch Shea and Sean and Noah get off. It all happens in this crazy kind of slow motion—no sound, except the weird ripping noise. And Noah walks across his yard, and then, just after my brothers disappear through our back door, my neighbor, Mr. Bowen, walks toward Noah. He leans over and points at something. I can't see what it is— it's something in the other direction. I go down the hill three or four steps to see where he's pointing. Mr. Bowen and Noah walk across Noah's yard, and I see them go around the side of Noah's house. And then they're gone, and so is the rip. It's not like the rip gets mended. It's just normal again. I stand there, numb.

"What are you doing, Gracie?" Mom opens the back door, a basket of laundry in her arms. She must've been in the basement doing laundry.

"M-m-m-m-m-m-m . . ." Uh oh.

"Gracie?"

I concentrate hard on making words. "Where's Dad?"

"Walking Sweetie. Baby, why are you outside? "

"Noah?"

"We didn't find him." She puts the basket down and steps outside to me. Even though it's still so early, there's a warm breeze blowing through the trees, and the stones on the path feel toasty under my bare toes. Mom wraps me in her arms. "Not yet. Hey," she adds as she pushes my wet hair off my face and kisses my forehead, "you're shaking, Gracie."

From the absolutely heavenly vantage point of my beautiful mother's embrace, I look back to Noah's yard, where I saw him disappear just seconds ago. And I see feathers on the grass, blowing away in the breeze.

I remember I never checked the drama club website last night. I don't know if I got a part in the play. And I haven't told my parents I tried out.

Right this moment, all I know is Mr. Bowen took Noah, and no one will ever believe me.

"It is only with the heart that one can see rightly; what is essential is invisible to the eye."
~ Antoine De Saint-Exupery

Chapter 7

I go upstairs and get dressed for school, and when I come down for breakfast, everybody's there. Outside the kitchen window, I see police cars, more than last night. Dad looks tired and upset. I grab a bowl from the counter, pour myself granola, and sit across from him.

It's like last night again when we ate dinner and watched the news. Eight of us are in the kitchen, and nobody talks. At all.

Finally, after about five minutes, Shea says, "What now?"

And then we all get crushed by silence again . . . until Sean starts to cry. Mom kneels on the floor next to his chair and wraps her arms around him. I realize my face is wet, and so I start grabbing breakfast dishes from everybody so I can at least try to hold it together. The last thing I want to do to Sean is totally unravel and make everything worse. Once I get to the sink, I lean on the counter, close my eyes, and breathe.

Mom gets up, walks to the counter, and pours coffee. She and I stand there and watch the police cars out the window. She puts her arm around me, and we rest our heads on each other.

"Hey, when do you find out if you got a part in the play?" Mom asks.

My sisters look at each other and leap up. They knock each other over, running into the family room.

I start to apologize to Dad for disobeying him, but he shakes his head.

"Gracie, good for you, baby. Your sisters said you were terrific."

"Where's the paper with the website?" Mary asks as they log on. I think back to what I was wearing at tryouts, trying to remember where I stuffed the piece of paper. I run up to my room. My pile of dirty clothes is gone. I run down to the basement, stumble over Sean's enormous stash of action figures, and step on Anakin, which hurts in bare feet.

"Hurry up!" Mary screams. "Gracie! Hurry up!"

I find my stinky, muddy sweatshirt, dig in the pocket, and pull out the slip of paper. For a heartbeat, I see a shadow move in the reflection from the overhead light on the washing machine. Chills tickle my backbone—that's twice in one morning. I force myself to turn around. I stand really still and scan the room. There's nobody here. I run back upstairs, fast, imagining someone will leap up and grab me as I'm trying to make my getaway, but if I can just close the basement door, I'll be safe, and all the monsters will stay in the basement. I get away.

Back in the kitchen, Dad is escorting Shea and Sean out the back door.

"You can see us from the window, Dad. This is dumb," Shea is complaining. Sean's not saying anything. I note he hasn't, all morning. I wonder if the boys saw Mr. Bowen when they got off the bus. I start to ask them, but Mary cuts me off.

"Gracie!!!" I remember I'm holding the paper with the drama club website.

While my sisters look it up, I walk to the kitchen window and watch Dad and the boys. I see other parents at the bus stop too. And the white-haired lady. I see her. She's standing apart from the others, looking from Noah's backyard to me. She sees me seeing her. Even this far away, I can make out the expression on her face. She's lifting her eyebrows, her white eyebrows, and leaning into me a little bit, like Mary and Bridget do when they're waiting for me to understand them. I can almost hear her ask, *So?* As I stand there, studying her, it hits me that she's not actually old at all—just white-haired. I squint to get a better look. Yeah, she's young all right. And *so* familiar.

Then Mary and Bridget are screaming and running into the kitchen. Mom puts her coffee down and looks from one to the other.

"You got the part!" Bridget says.

"What part?" Mom asks, laughing a little despite the heaviness in the room.

"You got Helen!" they say at once. I'm shocked. My mouth drops open.

Mom wraps me up in her arms. "Congratulations, baby."

"Here comes our bus," says Mary, and the three of us run out the door and down the hill, amidst all the parents and police cars.

I notice Julie Dunne isn't at the bus stop, and the white-haired lady seems to have left too. Julie usually sits in the seat behind me. I pass Hayden and take Julie's seat.

"Where's Julie?" says the girl who sits next to her. I shrug. I'm pretty sure Julie's been up all night with the rest of the neighborhood, looking for Noah. I open my mouth to say that, but nothing comes out. I can't talk about it. We pull out of our neighborhood.

Kids are talking about the police cars and what might have happened. My sisters and I don't say anything.

"You playing hard to get, Gracie?" Hayden says, sprawling out since he has our whole seat to himself. I don't know if his daily romantic advances are intended to make fun of me, or if on some level he's maybe insulted I'm not drooling over him. I don't know. It's a big mystery, really. I'm not the kind of girl that boys pay a lot of attention to. Bridget is. Mary is. I'm not. Pearl said Hayden was with someone at the Back to School Dance, and they seemed really hot and heavy. So why does he harass me every day? Sometimes when I look at him, I get glimpses of the boy behind the smirky mask. And that boy, I mean the boy people don't see—just seems lonely. Weirder yet, that boy, the lonely boy, seems to know I see him. And I have to admit, when I connect with *that* Hayden, even if it's for just a second, I like him. I like that Hayden a lot.

At school, a lot of kids have already heard a boy went missing, and I hear Julie's name in the halls. A few people I don't know congratulate me on getting Helen. The boy from auditions finds me at lunch.

"Hey," he says as he passes my table. "Read-through is today right after school in the drama room. I'm Marty. I'm AD. Congratulations. You did really well." He walks away, saunters really, and I turn back to my friends.

"What does AD mean?" Morgan asks.

"Grace, he's gorgeous," says Pearl. "And tall."

"Do you know what AD means?" Morgan repeats.

I look for him then—to figure out where he sits. Across the room, where most of the seniors sit, I see him. He's still standing, talking to the girl I auditioned with, Lisa. She stands on her tiptoes and kisses him. Ahh. Okay, I get it.

"He's taken," I tell Pearl.

After school, I go find Coach.

"I tried out for *The M-M-M*, the play," I start, really nervous. "And I got a part. So I'm-m-m . . ." I'm falling all over my m's.

"Grace, it's okay," she says in her squeaky little voice. "Your sisters said something, and I talked to the head coach. We haven't had any meets yet. So he said you can get your athletic fee back." She smiles like she means it. "Congratulations on the play."

"Thanks." I run upstairs to the drama room.

I don't actually have so much to do at the read-through. Helen only has one line in the show, "Wah wah." But it's really interesting to listen to everyone. Lisa got the part of Annie Sullivan, and she's outstanding. Another senior, Caroline, got Helen's mom, Kate Keller. And the boy who got the dad looks like a man, not a teenage boy. He's terrific too. My absolute favorite is the boy who got James Keller, an interesting character because there's more to James than you first think. I love that kind of character—someone with depth that you don't recognize at first. The boy playing James is Leo. He's in my public speaking class, and really shy here, I mean with these drama kids, probably almost as shy as me, but when he's reading he totally nails James' surly attitude. It's a fast two hours, and it's a relief to get caught up in it. It gives my mind a break from imagining what happened to Noah, which is all I've done all day. I love listening to the kids read. I picture the whole thing, and I think Ms. Dawson does too. The kids all call her Ms. D, and every once in a while, she stops them and talks about how she is visualizing how this or that will be on stage. It's fun to watch her talk. After the read-through, she gives me a book with an essay in it called "Three Days to See."

"Grace, I'd love for you to try to really get to know Helen, the woman she became. This is a wonderful essay about what she imagines she would do if she had three days to see."

44

I take it from her, feeling my face heat up. "Okay," I say, incredibly shy with this woman. Ms. D is young. I bet she's not even thirty. And she has this energy and charisma about her that I really like. I liked her the first time I met her.

"I'm delighted you auditioned, Grace. Thanks for being part of this."

I have no idea how to respond. She's thanking me? So I just smile and nod and keep my mouth shut, feeling like one of those crazy weeble wobbles people put in the back windows of cars.

Dad picks me up. He has Bridget and Mary with him. I'm guessing we won't be driving with teenagers until they find Noah.

"Any news?" I ask.

He shakes his head. "Not yet. But there's a boatload of police. And search dogs. And I'm guessing the men in black are FBI." My sisters laugh about Dad's use of the phrase, "men in black." I don't.

"I thought the FBI only gets involved when kidnappers cross state lines," I say.

"You watch too much crime TV," Bridget says.

Dad just shrugs.

As we get closer to the house, I see all the lights, just like last night, except there's even more.

"Can I help, too, Dad? Can I search with the people? If I stay with you?"

"Yeah, if you stay with me, baby."

And so Mom, Dad, and I join the neighbors. Sean and Shea wanted to search, but Dad said no, and he got pretty mad about it. We comb the woods around our house. We search ponds, barns, and an abandoned one-room schoolhouse that hasn't been used in a hundred years.

"Did M-M-Mr. Bowen help?" I ask Mom while Dad talks to police with some other parents in Noah's backyard.

"Who?"

"Our neighbor." I point to his house. It's dark. I wonder where the heck he is.

"Oh, right. Yeah, I'm sure."

"I didn't see him."

"What?"

"I didn't see M-m-m," I give up on saying his name, " . . . him. I didn't see him helping." I want to tell her what I saw this morning, how the sky ripped open, but I don't know how.

"What are you mad about, Gracie?"

"I'm not m-m-m . . . but where is he? Look, he's not home."

And just like that, like he heard me, he steps out of the darkness past where Dad is standing, and walks right up to us. He has a great big industrial-sized flashlight.

"Awful, huh?" he says. I imagine him standing in his bathroom and practicing facial expressions, figuring out which muscles create what appears to be a feeling, a feeling he doesn't really have at all. In the darkness, with all the flashlights casting crazy shadows, it literally looks to me like there are monsters surrounding him. I blink a few times. They're still there.

***

The humans search in all the wrong places. It grieves Clementine to watch them. It's like watching a bird, caught in a glass house, beating its wing against the transparent barrier, when a window is wide open just beyond its capacity to see.

She followed Bowen yesterday. She knows where Grace needs to go. What Clementine doesn't know is what he will do next to the boy he has trapped in the other place. Or what he would do to Grace if he knew she sees the demons that flank him. So Clementine watches him. She watches him hide things. The shadows that embrace him taunt her for her unwillingness to consume Grace the way the shadows consume the man.

"We play by different rules," she whispers.

"Rules that cost you the game," one says.

"My King already beat you at your game," she says, knowing she shouldn't even be engaging them.

And they laugh. They step closer to Clementine, smelling her fear. More of them arrive, and she discerns their features more clearly—their hungry eyes and quivering mouths, their sharp claws that cut when they touch. They're all different colors, sizes, and shapes, but every single one reminds her of something that's gone sour, rancid, bad. She unfurls her wings and pulls her sword from its sheath. They laugh louder and draw weapons of their own.

Despite her fear, Clementine lunges. She thinks about Noah, and in fury she screams out her God's name.

And they crawl away, into the man's house.

"What we once enjoyed and deeply loved we can never lose, for all that we love deeply becomes a part of us."
~ Helen Keller

Chapter 8

The FBI, local police, and search dogs seem a little less driven by the end of the second week. And maybe our parents are getting just a notch or two less vigilant too. Not because it's any less awful. It's just the way people are. Even my own dad, sometime around the middle of the second week, stopped escorting the boys to the bus stop. He stood, instead, at the window and watched them. I could look up from the high school stop and see him watching, but he stopped walking down the hill with them.

I still get this almost electric feeling in my bones when I turn the corner onto my street. It's like my body knows the bad thing happened *right here*, and if not for that impenetrable dimension of time, I could grab him back. Noah's picture is plastered all over town. I keep imagining someone walking out of a Wal-Mart or a 7-11, and looking at a picture of him and saying, "I've seen the boy on that flyer!" Then I imagine Julie's parents getting the phone call that Noah was found, and he's okay. And we're all celebrating.

It's Saturday morning. Dad, Mary, and Bridget are running with the cross-country team on the NCR Trail, Peter's home for the weekend getting Mom to do his laundry, and my little brothers are sequestered in the basement playing XBox. Nana is weeding when I step outside.

"Where are you headed, Gracie?" she asks.

"Running," I say.

"I thought you gave that up for the stage," she teases me.

"No, I love to run, Nana. I just wanted to be in the play too."

"Run by Papa Da's place if you can. I think he's a little down today."

I have a terrific playlist for running. All my favorite artists. Mainly girl bands. I pop in my earbuds and take off.

I run across Noah's backyard on my way to the footpath through the woods where I run and find myself in Mr. Bowen's backyard instead. I didn't plan it. It just happened. Still jogging, still listening to my girls, I travel a little closer to Mr. Bowen's house. I jog around front—the car's gone. I jog around back again and crouch down for a closer look into the basement. It's a sunny day, and I can't see anything inside the window because of the glare. So I cup my hands and press my face to the glass—and inadvertently open the window. I just push it in. So then I push the window all the way open and stick just my head in to get a better look.

Mr. Bowen teaches philosophy at Saint Anthony's, the college my brother Peter goes to. Peter has never had him as a teacher, but since he lives in our neighborhood, there are some things we know about Mr. Bowen. First, we know he doesn't have kids. We know he's single, at least now. I think Dad said he used to be married a long time ago. I'm not really sure, but the point is, if he does have some kind of extended family somewhere, none of us have ever seen them at his house. So I'm really curious as I look in the basement and see *lots* of Christmas presents all wrapped up. I mean lots. I mean, like, half the basement is covered. And Christmas is still three and a half months away. I'm kind of stuck in his window well when I think I hear a car pulling into a driveway—maybe not his, I tell myself. I pause my music. There's definitely someone here. I twist my head and fall back into his bushes. I crawl on all fours to put some distance between me and the basement, figuring I'll just act like I'm running through his backyard on my way to the footpath, when I remember the window is now wide open. A car door closes. I decide to forget the window. Let him wonder. I start running, and I don't look back.

Nana was right. Papa Da is sitting on the porch when I get to the center, just staring out the window. He looks all alone in the world. It makes me want to cry. I wonder where he is, in his head. Is he remembering Ireland, or his dead wives, or the days when he was free to go where he felt like going, even if that involved middle of the night bus trips?

"Hey," I say and lean over to kiss him on the cheek.

"Grace!" he says, lighting up. His one concession to English is names. Maybe there is no Gaelic version of Grace.

"I missed you, so I thought I'd run over." He smiles and reaches out to hold my hand. "I got a part in the play."

He nods, smiling like he already knows. I guess Nana told him, or maybe Dad.

"Co-gair-djas," he says, and then adds, "Oh muh anim," and he pats his heart.

When I learn more sign language, I'll have an easier time talking to Papa Da.

"Are you sad today?" I ask.

He nods and opens his arms to me. I'm tiny enough that I can fit on his chair with him. We have a nice, long hug. In his arms, I sense his yearning, his loneliness. I just don't know how to make him feel better.

"A boy in our neighborhood went missing," I say. "Noah. He's Sean's friend. You've m-m-m-met him lots of times. Sean's really upset about it. Me too. It's been almost two weeks now and still no clues. I'm afraid something bad happened."

He looks out the window again, the way he was looking when I got there. I think he's gone away in his mind when he looks back at me, and says, "Taw shee egg cween-idd," or so it sounds to me. Then he repeats it, like I'm supposed to memorize it, or write it down.

I nod and say, "Okay."

Then we drink tea and just sit. I tell him all about the Helen Keller essay. I promise to bring it with me next time I visit so I can read it to him. I think Papa Da would like it. Helen Keller describes all the things she would do if she could see for just three days. She talks about New York a lot—about the Empire State Building and the Metropolitan Museum of Art—things he would remember too. I didn't know before I read it that she had lived on Long Island when she grew up. I tell him that too.

"Taw shee egg cween-idd," he says to me again when I'm getting ready to leave.

"Okay, Papa Da," I say. He's trying to tell me something.

"Taw shee egg cween-idd," I whisper to myself as I run home. I'm not playing my iPod now. I'm afraid I'll forget his words if I do. I run past Mr. Bowen's. He's home, or at least his lights are on. I run past the Dunnes' house. There are a bunch of cars out front. Julie sees me and runs across the grass.

"We're having a prayer vigil tonight," she says. "Could you come?"

"Yeah." I want to say so much more to Julie. I want to tell her I'm praying all the time, every second, but God's not telling me anything back. I want to say that Mr. Bowen's basement is full of wrapped up Christmas presents in September. I want to tell her I saw him walking Noah away from his bus. But I nod instead, and just say "Yeah" again.

"Thanks, Grace."

The boys are still downstairs, and the girls still aren't home. Peter's snoring on the couch. I sit down at the computer and start scrolling down a page with Gaelic phrases.

"Taw shee egg cween-idd," I'm whispering. I read all kinds of phrases. They have "Above all else," and "Everyone has their opinion," and "It's a lovely day." But I don't see any phrases, any collection of words that would sound like "Taw shee egg cween-idd." Then I do. I read it. *"She is crying."*

She is crying? Who is crying, Papa Da? What does my great-grandfather know? I remember my white-haired lady friend on his cloud. *She* was crying. Does he see her too?

We hold a prayer vigil in the Dunnes' back yard, and it spreads out to free space on one side and Mr. Bowen's yard on the other. Father Mulcahy from Saint John's passes out candles, the kind my church uses on Christmas Eve. Once everyone is gathered, he starts to pray. I close my eyes. I feel less alone here—like maybe if we can carry all this grief together, it won't be so heavy. Lots of people pray out loud—people I didn't even know were spiritual. Mrs. Dunne prays, and then she starts to cry. She makes a terrible, heaving kind of wailing sound—I don't ever remember hearing a sadder cry in my life. Then Mr. Dunne and Julie start crying with her. The three of them hug each other for a long time, and sometimes one or the other's knee buckles, and I start worrying someone will collapse. I guess they're holding each other so tightly that they keep each other from falling down. It reminds me of a movie I saw. I can't remember the name, but in this one scene, this guy was talking about the power of family, and he had this pile of sticks. He picked up one stick and said that a person alone, without family to support him, had no strength when things got bad. Then he snapped it. But if a family can stick together, he said, they are invincible. He took a whole bundle of sticks and asked the other person in the scene to try to break the bundle of sticks, and that person couldn't do it. That's what Julie and her parents look like right now, a bundle of sticks, unbreakable because they're hanging on to each other. I'm standing there, in their backyard, holding my candle, blinking back the tears that keep blurring my vision. I'm standing in the same backyard where I batted piñatas and played hide and seek. If only I could wave my magic wand, and we could be at one of the Dunnes' Easter egg hunts. But I can't. And suddenly it's my voice sending up a prayer to God. I lift my face and ask God to find Noah now, tonight. I feel furious at Him, God I mean. I know my voice sounds angry as I pray, but I can't help it. I speak lots of "m" words in my prayer, and I don't think I stutter. I don't think I ever stutter when I talk to God. Then we all sing for a while. My little brother Sean says the last prayer.

"Bring Noah home." And he cries. I watch Mrs. Dunne hug him. I start to think about how she must be remembering all the things Sean and Noah have done together, all the memories she has of the two of them being together. But I can't think about it. It hurts too much. So I just try echoing my brother's prayer. "Bring Noah home," I whisper out loud.

And for the first time since it happened, I feel like God already did that—like Noah is home. But home isn't here . . . home isn't Earth. The realization, and the new wave of sorrow that follows, takes my breath away.

When it's over, and all the neighbors start to head back to their houses, I see Mr. Bowen talking to Dad. His vigil candle is still lit, and the flame lights up his face. I walk over to Dad and wrap my arm around him.

"Grace," Mr. Bowen says.

I nod.

He and Dad talk about the search and places they think the police should look more carefully. I feel like those shadows are hanging around him again, but this time I don't let myself look at them. I'm too busy looking into his eyes. He's holding his vigil candle near his face, and the reflected flames are burning inside his pupils.

"Did you see Noah get off the bus?" I ask him, cutting right into the middle of their conversation.

Dad and Mr. Bowen look at me.

"I ask because you were home. I saw your car," I add, lying. I didn't, actually, because *I* wasn't home. "So did you see him?"

"No," he says. The flames in his eyes dance. "Did you?" he asks.

Yes I did, I think to myself. *And I saw you.*

"The wings of angels are often found on the back of the least likely people."
~ Eric Honeycutt

Chapter 9

By the end of September, we've blocked the whole show, and we're starting rough run-throughs. I act mostly with Lisa and Caroline, but I'm slowly getting to know the other kids too. For the first couple of weeks, I didn't talk at all during rehearsal. Now I'm showing a little more of myself, which isn't exactly Chatty Cathy, but I'm feeling a little more like part of the group.

Kids who like drama are generally really different from kids who like to run. Runners, and more specifically long-distance runners, are usually quiet and smart. Actors, especially kids passionate enough to want to do non-musical dramas, are generally pretty smart too, but way more extroverted and flamboyant. One boy in the cast has five body piercings. Caroline has a tattoo of a musical note right in the small of her back. Leo, my shy friend who plays James, has dyed his hair three times already since school started. I feel like Milly Milktoast among them, but I like them. They're funny, and interesting.

Then there's Marty, the assistant director. Now that I'm a little more in the know, I've learned that it is very unusual for Marty to *not* be acting. He's apparently really talented. But he wanted to try his hand at the directing side of things. Knowing all this just makes me shyer with him. He looks like Leonardo DeCaprio when he was in *Titanic.* I keep waiting for him to jump up on stage during notes and scream, "I'm the king of the world!" So far, he's restrained himself. He's generally really nice to me, but I get a feeling he thinks I'm pretty ignorant. He's always quietly explaining things to me after Ms. D has given some kind of general direction. And after he explains something, he always gives me this smarmy wink. But he is helpful.

Today Ms. D talks about scene changes. She wants to minimize having kids on stage crew running out and changing set pieces too much. So she is trying to organize the cast to do some of the scene changes ourselves. I'm glad to do the work, but I feel dumb, as Helen, moving furniture around. I feel like, from an audience's point of view, that would look pretty funny. But I keep that opinion to myself.

So Ms. D is talking to me about striking a bench before the garden house scene. I'm on stage, and Ms. D is sitting halfway back in the auditorium. When she says "blackout", I'm supposed to strike the bench. She tells me I have thirty seconds to strike it, and then get into position. I'm confused, wondering why she wants me to hit the bench, but I'm about to do exactly that when Marty sidles over to me and whispers, "Strike means *take off stage*." And winks.

He has saved me certain humiliation, for which I'm thankful.

After rehearsal, I wander down to the girls' locker room and wait for my sisters on a bench outside. Caleb walks out of the boys' locker room door.

"Hey," he says.

I nod. "Hey."

"I saw you at the vigil." He sits down next to me. "Did you . . . I mean . . ." He shakes his head. "*Do* you know Noah?"

"We're neighbors. How about you?" I say. I sit on my hands, hoping I can hop around m-sounds if this conversation is going to last much longer.

"We're cousins," he says.

"Oh," I say. "Sorry. I didn't know."

"I liked your prayer." He bows his head, like he's either embarrassed or upset.

"Caleb, right?" I ask.

"Yeah," he says. He looks back at me. Then he kind of tilts his head to the side and squints a bit, like he's trying to remember. "Grace?"

"Yeah," I laugh.

"Gift from God."

"What?"

"Your name. It means 'gift from God'."

I nod. I have no idea what Caleb means, and I can't think of anything else to say.

A car pulls up. "See ya," he says and gets up to leave.

"Bye," I say.

I watch him walk to the car. He looks back and waves as he gets in. I consider our short conversation. I didn't stutter much at all.

I have just enough time after Caleb leaves to find a song on my iPod before Mary and Bridget come outside. Becca's driving us again. Dad's letting down his guard here too.

"Does anybody want to go to Saint John's with me tonight?" I ask as we barrel along in Becca's car.

"What?" says Mary. "Why?"

"No," Bridget says. "Not at all."

"I want to talk to the priest who led the vigil."

"Why?" Mary asks. Bridget doesn't wonder why because she's in the front seat, texting Tommy. I'm not sure if Bridget and Tommy are currently on or off. It's too confusing to keep up with her.

I shrug, hoping that will satisfy Mary. It does.

Mary and Becca start talking about who likes who on the cross-country team. Becca wants to fix Mary up with some guy, and they're plotting ways to make that happen.

"Bridget, the next pasta party is at our house. Did you remember that?"

They all start talking about pasta and dessert, who's fast, who's lazy, and good DVDs to watch. Becca pulls up the hill to our house.

"Hey Gracie, I live two blocks from Saint John's. Do you want me to give you a ride over there now?"

"Sure," I say.

All of a sudden, my sisters have lots to say about this.

"What are you doing there?" Bridget asks.

"Why are you going there?" Mary asks at the same time.

"I just told you," I say.

"No, you didn't," Bridget says.

"Who do you want to talk to?" Mary says at the same time.

They must think it's easy to listen to them talk in stereo.

"The priest at Noah's vigil."

"Why?" they ask, totally in unison. Kind of funny. You'd think they were twins.

I shrug. "Confession." It's the first lie that comes to mind. I know Catholics go to priests for confession.

"Confession?" Bridget looks irritated, getting out of Becca's car and dragging her book bag behind her.

"We're not Catholic, Gracie. Priests can't hear confessions of people who aren't Catholic," Mary says, suddenly the religion specialist. She gets out after Bridget, leaving me sitting there by myself.

"I just want to." They shake their heads, moan a little bit, slam the door, and disappear into our house.

I haven't planned exactly what I want to say to the priest, but all day I've been thinking about who I can get to help me, and I keep seeing his face. So I'm doing it.

"He's probably in the rectory," Becca says as we stop in the church lot.

"Where?"

"The priests' house."

I knock on the door, and another priest, one I haven't met, answers. I ask if I can talk to Father Mulcahy.

"Are you a parishioner?" He must know I'm not.

"No, but I was at the vigil for Noah Dunne, and . . . I have something I need to talk to him about."

"Come in," he says.

I wait in a nice, however colorless, room. I'm always surprised when I visit other people's homes and realize not everybody feels inclined to paint every surface a different color. It smells like frankincense here. And there are framed photos of priests on the walls. There's no piped-in muzak, but it feels like that would complete the effect.

Finally, Father Mulcahy comes into the room. I stand up, suddenly really sorry about this whole idea.

"Can I help you?" he asks.

"I'm Grace O'Shaunessy," I say, shaking his hand with my sweaty one. "I wanted to talk to you about Noah Dunne . . . about my neighbor." He releases my hand. There's something wrong with him—not Noah, but . . . my neighbor. His name's . . ."

"Sure," he says, cutting me off, and leads me out of this first room and into another one, this second one having more privacy, I guess. The two rooms look pretty much the same, except this second one also has a huge black and white picture of Jesus dying on the cross with Mary and some disciples crying at his feet. I'm taken aback for a second. It's gruesome, with Jesus' blood dripping through his fingertips, and it seems even more horrific hanging on a wall behind an expensive sofa covered in plastic.

"So the Dunnes are your neighbors?"

I'm rubbing my wrists, swallowing the acid rising in my throat and trying to push away feelings of big, heavy nails screwing Jesus to the cross.

"Oh, yeah. But I wanted to tell you about m-m-m-my other neighbor." I'm afraid if I don't just say it, I'll shut down. "M-m-my other neighbor lives next door to Noah, and I think he's the one who took Noah. He has about a hundred Christmas presents in his basement, and . . ." The priest's brow is getting all crinkled up.

"Do you mean Jason Bowen?" he asks.

I nod. At first it seems weird to me that he'd guess that so fast. Then I remember he was at the vigil and might know people in my neighborhood.

He opens his mouth to talk. "What did you say your name was again?"

"Grace."

"Grace, Jason Bowen wouldn't hurt a child." He smiles at me like he feels sorry for me because I'm so dumb. "Those presents are part of a toy drive."

He kind of nods then, like he wants me to say "Oh" or something. But I don't.

"We have a toy drive. With Saint Anthony's. Jason teaches there."

"I know. I know he teaches there. But I saw him . . . with Noah, the m-m-mmmorning," I plow through the word because I need this guy to stop smirking at me, ". . . the day after he disappeared. I m-m-m-mean, I saw this kind of . . ." I want to describe what I saw, how the neighborhood ripped in half and how I heard it, but the look on the priest's face shuts me down.

"I totally understand how sad you're feeling about Noah's disappearance. And I know you think you're doing the right thing here. But listen to me." He reaches out and holds both my hands. I guess it's supposed to be a gesture of comfort. I just feel cornered. "Let me tell you about Jason Bowen. This is a man who has been broken, and I mean broken, by tragedy in his life. And all he cares about now is doing God's work. You absolutely must not . . ." His tone gets a little creepy. "Do you hear me?" He stops and leans in closer. "You must not *slander* this man's good name. Do you understand me?"

"Yes," I say, disoriented. I thought I was following my intuition. I thought this priest would help me. He's still holding my hands. I try to let go. His hands touching mine make me feel like I'm in a room that doesn't have enough oxygen, like someone is sucking up all the good air. Collar or not, this guy is not such a good guy. Maybe not bad, but a lot blinder than Helen Keller.

"Yes," I say again. Then I do let go and stand up, desperate to leave. He stands up too.

"You have to trust the authorities. They'll find Noah Dunne. Right? What *you* can do is pray."

I just nod. I don't have any more words for this guy. I *am* praying. And I thought God said I should get a grown-up to help me. I thought this priest was the grown-up who could do that. I thought he was the answer to my prayer. He follows me as I back out of the room and down the hall to the front door.

"Do you need a ride?"

"No, thanks. I'm okay." I think about lying that I live nearby, but stop myself, realizing I already told him I'm Noah's neighbor. So he knows I live on the other side of town. What made me think I should go to Saint John's? I imagine this wisp of truth, and it's flitting around inside a bottle like a firefly in August, and Father Mulcahy is a great big cork, and he wants to trap it— the truth, I mean. But why? He wouldn't even listen to me.

As I walk back to the road, I hear music coming from the sanctuary, and what sounds like kids my age singing. Curious, and too worked up to just go home, I poke around until I find a way in.

I find a back door, and as I enter, I see some kids singing along with a praise band. It must be a practice or something like that. A few are standing with arms raised, eyes closed. The band keeps repeating the chorus, and more kids get up to sing.

After the song is over, someone starts a new song, and everybody sits. I'm thinking this would be a good time to leave, but when I recognize the opening chords of "Halleluia", the song from *Shrek*, I sit, too, in the back pew where nobody can see me. I crane my neck to see who's singing. It's Caleb. His voice is nice. He has his eyes closed, so I can watch him sing without him knowing I'm there. When he gets to the high notes, he goes into this sweet falsetto and raises his eyebrows a little bit, but he keeps his eyes closed until it's over. At the end of the song, I creep out the same back door, closing it as quietly as I can. For a quick second, I think he sees me, but it's so dark in here, just candles, I bet I'm wrong.

Then I run all the way home.

"Angels are never too distant to hear you."
~ Author Unknown

Chapter 10

Today is October 10th, Sean's eleventh birthday. Bridget and I get up early to make him chocolate chip waffles, his favorite breakfast. Not the frozen kind, but the kind with batter in the waffle maker and real chocolate chips. Mom gathers the rest of the family, and they serenade him in bed.

It's a fun morning. We're all trying a little extra this birthday. Sean's been quiet lately, ever since Noah disappeared. I mean, really quiet. Nana made cupcakes for him to take to school. Shea tried telling her that the kids don't generally have birthday cupcakes at lunch in middle school, but Nana told him Sean O'Shaunessy was only going to be turning eleven once in his life, and that was an occasion worth celebrating. That shut Shea up.

We're giving persuasive speeches this week in public speaking class. I've done better in this class than I thought I would. I can't manage the whole extemporaneous thing—I mean, I really have to write the speech word for word and make sure I'm not using any "m" words—so the impromptu speeches we give at the end of class have been a total bust, and pretty embarrassing. But for the big speeches, I've been picking topics I genuinely like, and I practice. So far I have an A. Today Leo is speaking. When he walks in, I notice he shaved his head to spell the word, *"Speak."* Funny guy.

When it's his turn to speak, instead of walking to the front of the room and putting note cards on a podium, he walks to the door. Zach, from the play, comes in, armed with a Styrofoam school bus that I think was a prop in last year's production of *You're a Good Man, Charlie Brown.* Zach leans the bus against the front of the podium, and Leo, who in the meantime has strapped on a little kid's book bag and donned a baseball hat, skips from behind the bus and waves at what I guess are his imaginary friends on the bus. I turn around and look at my teacher. He looks unruffled. This must be Leo's attention getter.

"Hey, kid," Zach says to Leo, "You want some candy?"

"Sure," Leo skips over to Zach, who is, by the way, a good six inches taller than Leo, and Zach grabs him, fast. Then he pretends to knock Leo out. Nothing at all happens for a moment.

One minute, I'm sitting in my chair, staring at them, and the next, I'm standing up in the aisle. I honestly don't remember getting up. I must've jumped up. I'm frozen, like a statue.

"Grace?" my teacher and Zach say at almost the same time.

"Oh. Sorry."

It might as well be Noah and Mr. Bowen, only it's the moment after they walked around the corner of Noah's house. I know that's what Mr. Bowen did—he grabbed him and knocked him out and has him hidden somewhere. I make myself focus. Leo gets up from the floor. He walks to the podium, fishing note cards out of a pocket. Zach nods to the teacher and leaves, bus in tow.

"Abductions," he says. "They happen all the time. Eight hundred thousand children younger than age eighteen are reported missing every year worldwide. Two thousand are reported missing each day." He waits for a second, like he wants to let the numbers sink in.

"It's easy to let numbers just bounce off the surface of your mind," he continues. "But to really think about two thousand children, every day, being taken is a nightmare. That's our whole school. My goal is to persuade you to, first, be more cautious yourselves, because even though we're in high school, there are still a lot of bad things that can happen to people our age. And my second goal is to get you to report anything you see that your good sense tells you to. If all of us paid more attention, a lot less bad stuff would happen. And maybe this is one of those speeches you'll remember one day way in the future, and you'll save a life."

It's a great speech. He talks about famous cases and how children were lured into cars. Adam Walsh was offered candy. Jaycee Dugard was waiting for her school bus. He talks about a boy in Miller Station, Maryland—and this is a case I don't remember hearing about, and Miller Station isn't far away. This boy, whose name was Keith Matthias, disappeared when he was only seven years old. He talks for a while about all the times people could've done something about what was happening in Phillip Garrido's backyard—that's the guy who took Jaycee Dugard. He talks about a really recent case. This nine-year-old girl, Aliahna Lemmon in Indiana, was brutally killed in a trailer park last Christmas by a guy who was supposed to be babysitting her. Leo asks us why we think nobody in the whole trailer park heard her screams. He's upset as he talks about it, and he compares people to ostriches. I'm upset too, mainly with myself.

I think about Noah, and where he might be. If I'm wrong about Mr. Bowen, where's Noah? I think about the Christmas presents in the basement. I've got to get into his basement and rip them open. I realize I'm picking at my fingernails when I pick too close to my skin and start bleeding. Ahhh, it burns.

Finally, in Leo's conclusion, he gives us all a piece of paper and asks us to write down one single thing we know that we're not telling people, a thing that could do good if only we would speak, if we could manage to get our heads out of the holes we're hiding in. I write, "I saw Mr. Bowen take Noah." I have tiny handwriting to begin with, and I write this really small and then cover it with my hand. My hands are shaking, a lot. Leo looks at us and says, "Now go tell someone, and save a life." Before he sits down, he turns around and shows us his shaved word, "Speak." Not so funny anymore.

I think about Leo's speech for the rest of the day. I have public speaking in the morning, so it's a long day.

At rehearsal, Lisa and I are working on the last scene. Ms. D calls it Helen's epiphany. I'm trying to find that feeling of discovery inside me as we practice. We're at the water pump, and Annie is making me fill the pitcher, steadfastly trying to teach me to fingerspell. I desperately want to discover the memory of water inside of me, inside Helen, and not just move to the next moment in the play. I feel like I owe Helen Keller more truth than that. I'm thinking about memory, about buried memories, and how it would feel to dig deep down and find a vital one. I make myself think about my scary dream, the one where I'm flying away from Earth and I can't speak because I . . . because I saw something, and it scared me, so I buried it. I go through the motions, and everybody seems pleased, but I know I'm not there yet. I know what scares me is still buried.

We all go out to dinner for Sean's birthday. We pick up Papa Da and go to Angelo's, Sean's favorite Italian restaurant. There are nine of us tonight, everybody except Peter, who Dad thinks could've made it if he tried. We have fun. We talk about races and movies, and Dad tells some hilarious stories. Papa Da keeps saying, "Knee higg-im!" and then he folds his arms and laughs too. The waitress brings birthday cake, and we embarrass my baby brother in good form with a loud rendition of "Happy Birthday."

At some point, someone broaches the subject of Noah. Bridget says she has something she wants to talk about, something she and Mary have been thinking would help.

"I think we should organize a 5K for the Dunnes, to raise money." We all look at her. "Mary thinks it's a good idea too."

"Do they need money?" asks Nana.

"Sure!" says Bridget.

"For what?" asks Shea.

"Well, I don't know. Lots of things . . ." Mary takes a breath and Bridget picks up the thread.

"Mr. Dunne hasn't gone back to work. So is he still getting paid? Isn't he self-employed?" Bridget says.

"Maybe they could get a private detective," says Mary.

"Aren't the police still investigating?" Mom asks.

"I haven't seen any police around the neighborhood in weeks," says Shea.

"Did they give up?" asks Sean. Everyone looks at him. That's the first thing he's said since we got to Angelo's.

"No," Dad says, "but it certainly couldn't hurt to have more people snooping around. The answer's somewhere. Girls, I like your idea. I'm in."

"Me too," Sean says.

Back home, I find Mom after everyone else has settled in for the night. I'm working on a theory I have brewing in my head about Mr. Bowen.

"Do you remember when I started to stutter?"

"What?"

"When I started to stutter."

"Gracie, what do you mean?"

"Do you remember an event?"

"When I first noticed, honey?"

"Yeah."

We're in the basement. Mom is sorting socks, a challenging task for a mother of six. She has baskets for each of us, so right now she's just studying socks and tossing them in baskets. I grab mine and try matching the singletons up.

"I guess so."

"Can you tell me about it?"

"Now?"

I nod, and she tosses me an assortment of crazy-colored ones.

"You had a seizure of some kind, um, a fit."

"Yeah?"

"Yeah."

"And?"

"And? And what?"

"Details. Where were we? How old was I? That kind of stuff."

"At the playground. The one here in the neighborhood. I think you were trying to call me. You were making a noise like . . ." She presses her lips together and hums. It's the sound of my dreams. "You didn't talk at all for a couple of months after that. It was awful. Dad and I took you to Johns Hopkins because we were scared that you had some form of epilepsy. But . . ."

"But I didn't?"

"No, you just had that one . . . episode."

"How old was I?"

"Um, five I guess." She strains to make sure that's right. "Yeah, it was on September 11th."

"Who else was there?"

Mom thinks for a moment. "All of us. Or, no. Gracie, I'm not sure. Why do you want to know?"

I study her as she talks to me. Mary has Mom's elegance, and Bridget has her beauty. I wonder what I have. Probably her nervous disposition. And maybe a touch of her spunk.

"Who else was there? Anyone else we know? That you remember?"

She considers this last question. She starts to shake her head. "I don't think so honey."

"Do you think M-M-M-Mr. Bowen could've been there?"

At first, Mom seems about to say no, like she's certain. But then she stops herself. I watch her face—her eyes go back in time. When she comes back to me, she's surprised.

"You know, I think he was. Huh. I wonder if he remembers that. Sure, because I used his cell phone to call 9-1-1. I didn't have one of my own— that's how long ago it was."

"I think he kidnapped Noah."

"Gracie!"

"What if he scooped him up right when Noah got off the bus and has him locked away in his house or someplace else, and we're all just walking around like the people in California?"

"Why would you . . ."

"You know, Jaycee Dugard. The girl who lived in tents for years. And people *lived* in that neighborhood . . ."

"Gracie! Stop! Jason Bowen is *not* a kidnapper."

"How do you know?"

She studies me, like she's deciding something. "Just trust me," she says.

I have the paper from class in my jeans pocket. I go upstairs. My sisters are both asleep. After I wash my face and brush my teeth, I get into my bed and twist on just one of my Christmas lights. I hold the paper and read it to myself, keeping my words inside my head. "I saw Mr. Bowen take Noah."

I make a vow to God, and to my white-haired lady who I haven't seen since she told me to find Noah. I will find him, and I will make sure Mr. Bowen doesn't hurt anybody else. The priest didn't believe me, but somebody will. I think about evidence and the "answers" Dad talked about. What is it they call it on the crime shows? Corroborating evidence. Isn't that what an expensive detective would look for? That's what I have to find if I want someone to believe me—evidence. Noah had his book bag with him. That has to be somewhere. The first thing I have to do is get inside Mr. Bowen's house. Then I'll find out what's inside all those presents. Before I talk to any other adults, I'll find proof. That's my next step. I have to show them something. I close my eyes, and think I see a feather float by the window, but that could be me dreaming.

"I am only one; but still I am one. I cannot do everything, but still I can do something; I will not refuse to do something I can do."
~ Helen Keller

Chapter 11

It's Homecoming Week. Our theme this year is "Starry Nights", and last Friday we all stayed after school and decorated. Morgan and I are both pretty decent artists. The freshman advisor must've done some snooping to learn that because we both got personal invitations to stay after school on Friday and help. I would've stayed anyway. My sisters would've made me. But it was good for Morgan to feel invited.

Bridget was helping to build some kind of huge New York City skyline in the junior section. The juniors were imagining a starry night in Manhattan, I guess. Mary was one of dozens of seniors who were staying after. This year's senior class is really competitive. They've made it their mission to win every Homecoming Week contest. So for their hall decorating, they're hanging Christmas lights all over the lockers, door frames, and ceiling tiles. Mary tried to snag mine, but I said no way, José. I guess the seniors were going for the world's starriest night.

So Morgan and I drew lots of different-sized stars and cut them out while other kids hung them all over our section. It was kind of a literal expression of "Starry Night," but by the time we left, it looked pretty.

So today, Monday, is Decade Day. That means we get to wear fun outfits from the 1950s through the 1980s, depending on what grade we're in. My sisters put a lot of time into today's outfits. I didn't do much—I just wore what they told me to. The freshmen got the 1950s. At first, I thought I could wear jeans and a white tee shirt and say I was a greaser. But Bridget said that was a lazy idea. Thinking about it more, I thought it might be nice to look girlier. Maybe I'd run into Caleb. So I let them put me into a pink poodle skirt with a white blouse and a super-high ponytail. Oh yeah, and I have on what is probably twenty-year-old pink lipstick. It feels like glue on my lips.

Mary looks like Madonna in the "Like a Virgin" video. I hope she doesn't get called down to the principal's office because Mom won't enjoy having to get herself a substitute so she can fetch Mary more modest clothes.

For the 70s, Bridget borrowed Mom's wedding dress. It's yellow with orange and pink flowers. The six of us kids all have a theory that Mom and Dad must've been hippie- wannabes. I say wannabes because my parents got married in the nineties, not the seventies. But anyway, back to Bridget in Mom's dress—she looks really pretty in it.

Hayden, on the other hand, who's a junior, does *not* look good in his get-up at all. And I hope he *does* get a referral. Talk about awkward. When I get on the bus, I see him sitting there, just waiting for me to sit next to him, and I feel ill. He's wearing spandex everything—with a dumb terrycloth headband pushing his bushy eyebrows into a perpetual scowl. All his hairy body parts are poking out everywhere, and the outline of his private parts is appallingly evident.

"Isn't that more eighties?" I ask him.

"It can be whatever you want it to be," he says.

I look past our seat to Julie. She's not dressed for Decade Day, but she does look entertained that I have to sit next to a pornographic version of the younger, hotter John Travolta.

I look out the window, and there's Mr. Bowen, gardening at 7 a.m. He must know I'm waiting for him to go somewhere because he's suddenly in his yard, weeding or raking or reading 24/7, literally. I wonder if he got fired from his teaching job. I'll have to ask him.

On the bus, I manage to stay on my side of the invisible line between Hayden and me, even when the bus driver makes sharp turns. I hang on to my seat cushion like my life depends on it.

The hall decorations are a big hit, especially the senior section. The best part of the day, really, is walking to and from classes, and the first few minutes in a new class, seeing what everybody looks like. In public speaking, a junior is giving a persuasive speech on legalizing marijuana, and she's dressed like Janis Joplin, who, I believe, actually *died* of a drug overdose. Probably not such a credible look, given the goal of her speech. But that's part of the fun of Homecoming Week. My art teacher has a senior advisory, so he's teaching about impressionism while wearing a wig that makes him look like he has a mullet. My English teacher is dressed like Bob Dylan, whom he actually looks like quite a bit—I mean, every day. Everybody's just kind of doing his or her normal thing, dressed funny.

In lunch, Pearl tells Morgan and me about a boy in her freshman seminar class who asked her to the Homecoming Dance. Nobody asked Morgan or me, unless you want to count Hayden. He asks me daily if I have a boyfriend yet and assures me he could make himself available—even if it meant breaking some hearts. He even said that if I find, in twenty or so years when I'm all grown up, that I'm an old maid, he'll marry me. I think he's making fun of me, but with him it's hard to tell.

"Guys, are you mad at me? I mean, I know we were all going to go together and do dinner and everything." Pearl looks concerned.

Morgan does actually seem a little miffed. I'm not, though. Maybe I'm more used to plans changing when boys call. I have two older sisters. Morgan's an only child. Plus, if Caleb asked me to the dance, regardless of dinner plans, I'd say yes in a heartbeat.

"What's his name?" I ask.

"Scott."

"Scott what?" Morgan asks. She's all of a sudden interested.

"Scott Brandt . . . I think that's it. I know it's a one syllable name."

I'm nodding and smiling and wanting details. I'm about to ask Pearl what he looks like. I look across the table at Morgan. She's holding her peanut butter and jelly sandwich in mid-air, like she forgot to eat it.

"He didn't go to our middle school," Pearl says, "so we didn't —"

"Yes, he did," Morgan says, her voice sounding flat.

Now Pearl and I are both uneasy.

"He moved here in the spring. I guess you just never noticed him." She finishes her lunch and gets up. Pearl and I look at each other.

"What's wrong with her?" Pearl asks me.

I shrug ignorance, but I'm guessing Morgan likes this Scott guy. Morgan's more like me than Pearl. Pearl is tall, blonde, and pretty. Her family has lots of money to buy her all kinds of nice clothes. She doesn't ever worry that anyone might find her . . . inadequate. But Morgan is a train wreck with boys. If she liked this Scott guy last year, I'll bet he didn't have the slightest idea. Or worse, he thinks she hated him.

At rehearsal, we start with a twenty-minute warm-up. Ms. D wants everyone to understand how it would feel to be deaf and blind. So she passes out earplugs and blindfolds and tells us we'll be taking a trust walk around campus. She hands some of us stopwatches and tells us they're set for twenty minutes, and we should push start as soon as we take off. It occurs to me we won't be able to see or hear our stopwatches, so I program the alarm function on my phone and set it to vibrate. Before we plug our ears and don our bandanas, she says that, short of certain calamity, we are not to remove these "sensory deprivers", as she calls them, for the full twenty minutes.

"Bonus points for the person who comes back with the most sensory details!" she calls out brightly. "I mean, details from the senses you've still got."

She maneuvers us around like a deck of cards until every other one of us has his or her right hand on someone else's shoulder. I wasn't a stopwatch holder, so I'm assuming my partner is. I have my right hand on some much taller person's shoulder. Then I feel my partner patting down my hair and my face, probably trying to figure out who I am. I can tell by his touch that it's a boy. So I do the same to him. I'm pretty sure it's Zach. I recognize him by the feel of his hair. Well, that's a relief. He's our resident man-boy—a grown-up man trapped in a boy's body. He's too responsible to let me go careening down a flight of stairs. At least, I hope so.

So we're off. Still wearing my poodle skirt, I travel along with Zach. We take baby steps out of the auditorium, into the hall, and toward the door to the senior patio. We grope along, leading with our hands. We make our way through the heavy glass door to the outside. This is actually a really cool exercise. I've never been so aware of how the air feels against my skin. It's overcast today, but I can still feel a little warmth when the sun peeks out from behind a cloud. We slow down when we think we're close to the steps that go down to the football field. And all of a sudden, I lose Zach. His big shoulder is gone, replaced by air.

"Zach?" I say, probably too loudly because of the earplugs in my ears.

I feel hands catching me as I lose my balance and go flying forward.

"Zach?" I say again, louder. I poke my fingers into somebody's eye sockets and this someone, who clearly doesn't know the rules of this exercise, pulls my bandana down to the bridge of my nose.

"Blah blah blah," Caleb says, or so it sounds to me with these earplugs jammed in my ears. He's smiling at me, dressed in a tee shirt and gym shorts—which is how you know he's an underclassman. Most of the upperclassmen guys on the cross-country team insist on wearing short-shorts all the time. And I'm kind of wrapped around him, for a moment anyway.

By now, Zach is back. I want to skip the rest of this exercise and just stand here in Caleb's arms, but Zach is blindfolding me again.

"See ya," I say, or scream, to Caleb. He's laughing. He waves. I guess he figured out I can't hear him.

Deaf and blind again, and hanging on to each other, Zach and I head back inside the school. I'm not taking any more chances. All the way back in, I keep replaying that moment—how it felt, the look on Caleb's face, the way he held me.

Ms. D wants everyone to talk about the trust walk before we rehearse. Lots of kids do. Not me, though. As I pretend to listen to the others, I'm still back on the patio, feeling Caleb catch me.

My sisters find me midway between the auditorium and the girls' locker room after their practice and my rehearsal. They're bickering about whether or not we should use ribbons or medals for Noah's 5K. Coach loved the idea. Mary and Bridget pitched it to her and the whole team the day after Sean's birthday. So they're now into the "organizing of details" stage. We have the run scheduled for the first Saturday of November. Everybody's hoping Noah will be home by then, but . . .

I join them, and the three of us walk home. Dad's working late, so he can't pick us up, and Becca got her car confiscated because she smashed it into a teacher's car in the teacher's lot.

"What about a tee shirt design?" says Bridget, as we start over the footbridge.

75

"I like Mom's design. It's a clear message. It should be simple," says Mary.

"But it makes me think of Amnesty International. Isn't that plagiarism, or some kind of copyright infringement?" asks Bridget.

"Amnesty International has a bunch of candles, Bridget. This is different. It's just one. I like it. One candle expresses hope," Mary says.

"Why can't we just say 'Run for Noah'? Why do we need a picture on the shirt?"

I'm walking behind them, trying to figure out what I think about all this. I love the idea of helping the Dunnes—and I guess money is a means to an end. I think about a tee shirt with a picture of Mr. Bowen snatching Noah as he's getting off his bus and a caption that says, "Arrest this Man." I don't suggest it.

We're halfway over the footbridge when I start feeling like someone's watching us, like there's somebody below us looking up at us. I stop and peer through the holes in the wire fence lining the edge of the bridge. I see something, some movement. And it smells weird too—like someone just lit a match. Below the footbridge is a stream, and then, further away, a highway. Bordering the stream is woods. Somebody was just there, in the woods.

"Grace." Mary and Bridget are pretty far ahead.

"Hello?" I say, sticking my face close to the chain link fence so I can see better. "Hello?"

"Grace! Who are you talking to?" They're annoyed.

I jog to catch up. "There's someone under the footbridge."

"Okay," says Mary. "And?"

"Let's go see who it is."

"Why?" asks Bridget.

"I'm going to go see," I say and run ahead, figuring that gives them no option but to follow. When I get to the bottom of the footbridge, I take the dirt path to the stream, walking sideways as I go down the hill and into the woods. Mary and Bridget aren't coming. A week ago, it'd still be light out. Tonight, it's dark, and not even 6 o'clock.

"Gracie! What the *hell* are you doing?" asks Bridget, or maybe it's Mary. It's hard to tell.

"Hello?" I say. We see each other at the same time. He's a kid, my age maybe. He's about fifty feet away from me, standing totally still—like a rabbit. He has some kind of bag, like a trash bag, and he looks like maybe he was about to dump its contents into the stream. The only thing about him I can see clearly are the whites of his eyes. They're huge.

"What's in the bag?" I ask.

He doesn't answer. He just backs away, toward the stream. Then he runs. He crosses the stream by climbing across a bridge of rocks. By the time he gets to the other side, I've gotten to the stream, and I'm starting across after him. I'm not sure why I'm following this kid.

Once he's on the other side, he really runs, still holding his great big trash bag. Busy watching him and the way he's holding the bag, not like it's trash but like it's got something important in it, I miss a rock and fall into the water. By the time I'm standing again, pink poodle skirt dripping muddy water, the kid has gotten into a car that must've been parked along the shoulder of the highway. I see something in the grass on the other side of the stream. I jump across the last couple of rocks and lean over to pick up some crumpled Christmas wrapping paper.

"Grace!" My sisters are standing on the other side of the stream, hands on hips.

"That kid . . . he had something in a bag . . . he was about to dump it in the stream. It could . . ." I was thinking about Noah . . .

"Who are you now, Gracie? I thought you were Helen Keller. Are you Nancy Drew now?"

"This Christmas paper—it's from Mr. Bowen's house." I hold it up to show them as I cross the stream.

This time they don't say anything, just look sideways at each other.

"Yeah, I know that sounds kind of random, but . . ."

"Let's go home," Mary says as my sisters start back toward the road.

After a sufficient pause, intended to let me know what a freak I am, they discuss Decade Day. They talk for another mile about all the clothes they liked and didn't like, what was in good taste, what looked awful.

"Did anyone mind your exposed tummy?" Bridget asks Mary.

Mary shakes her head. "Just goes to show, little sista', how flawed the system is. I could be dressed like Lady Gaga, and I'd get away with it. Why? Because I'm in NHS, and because I'm a jock."

This opens up a new can of worms, and now they're discussing tomorrow's Celebrity Day outfits. Mary is going to be Taylor Swift and Bridget wants to be Bella from *Twilight*. Bridget's talking about covering herself with glitter, and Mary's saying Bella doesn't shimmer until she becomes a vampire at the end of the series.

"How about you?" Mary asks me.

"Milkmaid," I say.

"Good one, Gracie," says Mary. "Such celebrities milkmaids are these days."

I stick the wrapping paper in my pocket.

"You're in the arms of the angels. May you find some comfort here."
~ Sarah McLachlan

Chapter 12

Today is Homecoming Friday. We have a pep rally last period, so the whole day is pretty frenzied. My class is at a distinct disadvantage. None of us really knows the cheers we're supposed to yell at the top of our lungs, except the freshman cheerleaders, and they've got troubles of their own. It's mainly the freshman girls who get put on top for all the stunts, and I feel like an awful lot of them keep toppling off. Scary to watch.

When we first sit down, I'm pretty surprised by how small a school we seem to be. I've never seen the whole school together in one place before, and there are a lot fewer of us than I expected. Today is school color day. We're the Butler Bald Eagles, and our colors are really just black and gold, but we throw in white, too, so we have three colors for Spirit Week. So today the freshmen are in white, the sophomores wear black, the juniors are in gold, and the seniors wear all three colors. With us all separated by color, the bleachers in between look empty. Then the Athletic Director starts introducing sports teams, and I realize all those kids on the teams aren't here, and that's why our student body looks so tiny. As each team is introduced, they do a funny dance that's choreographed to music. The soccer players and girls' field hockey team are hilarious. The cross-country team runs in to the theme from *Chariots of Fire.* The boys' and girls' team captains have flames like they do at the Olympics, except ours are battery-operated. Still, I love it. I see Caleb. He looks embarrassed, and that makes him look cuter. By the time all the teams are in the gym, the stands are full.

They announce the runners-up for Homecoming Court. Marty and Lisa are nominated for King and Queen. They remind me of Barbie and Ken as they walk across the gym.

Clothes-wise, today was the easiest day all week. Monday, I was itchy and sticky in my fifties' outfit. Tuesday, I felt self-conscious and pretty constricted in my milkmaid dress that Mom made for me when I was twelve.

And everybody kept asking me all day what celebrity I was. I should've listened to my sisters.

On Wacky Wednesday, Bridget braided all our hair in six or seven braids each, and then stuck wires in them to make our hair stand up like antennae. By the end of the day, I had an awful headache from wires poking into my head. Thursday was pajama day, which sounds uncomplicated, but I don't actually own any pajamas. I'm more of a tee shirt and sweatpants girl. So my choices were Peter's oversized plaid flannel pajamas—and he's a lot taller than me—or one of Bridget's itchy nighties, which are all too girly-girl for me to ever wear in public. I wore Peter's pajamas and spent the whole day hitching up my pant legs. So today I'm wearing white sweatpants and a white tee, and I feel great.

At the end of the pep rally, they announce the winners of all the different contests. The sophomores win the spirit link contest. That involved buying paper links and hanging them around the halls. Admittedly, I didn't buy a single one. The seniors win hall decorating, and they also win for their loud cheering at the pep rally. The juniors win the pie-eating contest. We don't win anything. I think the whole thing's fixed. Every time the cheerleaders start a new cheer, and the judges pick the loudest class, the freshmen have to cheer first. And we're all sitting there, this sea of fourteen-year-olds in white, looking around like idiots because we just don't know what to do.

At rehearsal today, we actually run the whole show—from beginning to end. I learn a lot about Helen today. There's a huge difference between trying to step into Helen's world for a scene, or ten minutes. Today, I'm Helen for two whole hours. Even when I go offstage, instead of going out in the hall or outside to get fresh air, I find a chair in the corner backstage and stay with Helen. I remember flip books from when I was a little kid. There'd be a whole stack of pictures, and if I flipped through them really quickly, they would blend together and become one single moving image. That's what it's like to be Helen for a whole two hours. All the separate Helens—the temper tantrum Helen, the naughty Helen, the dining room Helen, the good girl Helen in the garden house, and the last Helen, the Helen who speaks—they all mesh into one little girl today.

During notes, afterward, Ms. D talks about love, and what it does to people. She says all these characters—even Helen's bitter half-brother

James—love her, but they can't reach her. She's buried in another world. Annie is the miracle worker because she dives into that world and fishes Helen out. It's a cool image, and I think about it a lot. She asks everyone to journal this weekend. She jokes that she knows it's homecoming weekend, but she wants us to take a few moments for *The Miracle Worker*. She wants us to journal about what we would do for love. How deep into icy water would we swim to reach someone? I finger the Christmas paper in my sweatpants pocket. I've been putting it in pockets all week.

Dad picks me up tonight. Bridget and Mary got a ride to a pasta party. They have a meet in the morning. Dad asks me about my day. I ask him about his. I plug my iPod into the car radio and play music I think he'll like.

"Can you go to the meet tomorrow?" I ask.

"Yeah. You?" he says.

"Yeah," I answer. "Where is it?"

"Hagerstown," Dad says.

I figure I'll bring *To Kill a Mockingbird* with me. It seems like a wonderful book, but I'm way behind in class. Every time I try to concentrate, my mind wanders to Noah or Mr. Bowen or Helen or . . . Caleb.

Dad and I ride in silence for a bit.

"Are you going to the dance tomorrow night?" he asks after a moment.

"Sure," I say.

School dances aren't a safe subject for Dad and me. I was really excited about the eighth-grade dance last spring. Mom made me a dress. She has all kinds of talents, that woman. And I loved it. I figured I would get to wear something beautiful and unique. Anyway, when I got there, ninety percent of the girls looked a lot more . . . *mature* in their dresses than I did in mine. And they acted more mature too. That was the first time I saw kids grinding, and these were only thirteen- and fourteen-year-olds. I stood there in my homemade dress, looking like I was making my First Holy Communion, and didn't move from that spot, really, until my dad picked me up three hours later. My friend Pearl, true to form, had snagged a date. His name was Bernabé. He played the French horn in the eighth-grade band. Pearl plays flute. He's gone now. I think his parents were in the United States illegally.

They were from El Salvador, and one day they were just—gone. But he was a nice kid. He and Pearl didn't grind. They just danced.

I think Morgan went, but as I recall, she didn't stay long. She got sick, I think, and left really early.

So I was pretty much alone.

And when Dad picked me up, he wanted to know how many boys had asked me to dance. I shook my head and said, "None", but he couldn't believe it. In my dad's eyes, I'm what every boy dreams of, and his incredulity was merciless.

"None? None? Are you kidding me? Not one boy asked you to dance?"

By the time we got home, I was mad at Dad instead of at anybody else.

On Saturday we drive to the girls' meet, but they're not in the car because they took the bus from school with the rest of the team. I'm thinking Caleb will be there too. Dad goes over the Catoctin Mountain instead of taking Route 70. He thinks it's faster. My brothers and I disagree. We think he just prefers the scenery. I'm studying peoples' Halloween decorations along the roadside instead of reading my book. Anyway, it's too hilly for me to read.

Decorating for Halloween has turned into a major American pastime. People have scarecrows hanging from nooses on tree limbs and headstones on front lawns with hands sticking out of lumps of dirt. There's a plethora of black cats and ghosts. One house has a casket on the front lawn with some mechanized cadaver sitting up and waving as we drive by. The creepiest one is this random house, farther back from the road, with no decorations at all. It has a garage with dirty contact paper peeling in the windows, and a stone well on the front lawn that looks like it has to be two hundred years old. It makes me feel cold inside. Goosebumps march across my arms, and the hairs on my arms stand up.

I really love cross-country meets. I love running around the course, cheering on runners from bunches of different spots. I think it's a lot more exciting than watching people run around a track.

It's getting to be late in October, and it's kind of chilly out today, cool enough for a hat. I'm bundled up and waiting for the first race to start. We don't know any of the junior varsity boys running it, but it's a good chance to learn the course. And Dad and I are active spectators who like to scream.

Caleb runs in the varsity boys' race. That must mean he's fast because I'm pretty sure he's just a sophomore. I cheer for him, but I'm shy about being too vocal. And there's a girl here—I think I remember seeing her at Saint John's the night he was singing—with a huge "Go Caleb" sign. Maybe she's his sister. He does well. His time is 17:32, which is a terrific time for a boy, especially a sophomore. After his race, I try to find him in the crowd before the girls line up, and I see the girl with the sign before I see Caleb. She runs over to him, tosses down her enormous sign, and plants a kiss on his lips. I just stand there. Then I turn around and go find Dad.

I'm pretty shocked. I must not be such a great judge of nonverbals after all. I really thought Caleb acted like he liked me, at least a little. I feel embarrassed, dumb, and just plain depressed. I bump into lots of people as I try to work my way back to where Dad is standing, muttering apologies and trying to bounce back in my own head, but I keep seeing that girl kissing Caleb. Dad sees me and waves. I wave back.

Bridget is excellent today. She runs in 19:40. Her goal had been to break twenty minutes. She's thrilled. She takes third place for the whole race, which is really good for our school. That means a lot of points for us. Mary starts out strong, too, but somewhere in the woods, she must have fallen down or something because when she re-emerges, she's way back in the pack. Her knee is bleeding, and she looks really winded as she crosses the finish line. Her time is 25:56, which is a really slow time for Mary. I think it might be the worst time she's had since her freshman year. I'm not sure, but I know Dad knows. He keeps file folders on this stuff. He's such an accountant. While Tommy is hugging Bridget, Mary walks off by herself. Mom goes after her, and I can see her crying in Mom's arms. I know it's going to be hard for Mary to be glad for Bridget. They're both just so darn competitive, especially with each other. It would be so much easier if one was a great musician, and the other was a math whiz. But it's not like that. They always have their eyes on the same prize. Things are especially ugly when the prize is a boy.

We stay for the awards ceremony. The top eight get ribbons, so Bridget gets one, which is just one more thing for Mary to stew about. I can see the back of Caleb's head. He's sitting with the team. The girl who kissed him isn't with him, and I don't see her in the stands, but there are hundreds of people here. The girls catch the bus home with the team, and the rest of us pile back into the minivan.

Dad and Shea are playing "Name that classic rock tune", a favorite made-up game of my brother Seamus. He prides himself on his knowledge of the music of Led Zeppelin, the Rolling Stones, Jefferson Airplane, the Beatles—anything at least thirty years old, I guess. If my parents have it in their musty collection of record albums, Shea O'Shaunessy knows it. The second a song starts, he's naming the band. The opening chords of "Hell's Bells" grace our collective ears, and Shea screams, "AC/DC!"

I fall asleep in the backseat with my head resting on Nana's shoulder. I wake up and slam my head into the armrest.

"Gracie! Why'd you do that?" Nana asks, cradling my head.

I was dreaming. I was floating someplace—some rainy place. And there were shadows. I couldn't see what the shadows were at first, but then I could see that they were children. They were all hiding. They were trying to hide behind the raindrops. And the claws I remembered from other dreams were just fingers. I watched them turn into fingers, a man's fingers reaching to grab me.

I look out the window, and it's raining. Maybe that's why I dreamed about rain. We're back in the world of macabre lawn ornaments. I massage the bump forming on my forehead.

***

Clementine weaves images, whispering them across the breeze.

She watches the car pass one way, and then, hours later, the other. She is perched atop the well, afraid to go inside the house or into the water below. She starts down a few times, but halts, afraid to jump. Finally, she lets go of the wall and falls, far down. She reaches the bottom and splashes into the cold, stagnant water. And sees what she knew was here.

84

Inside the house, the man is here, with the boy. Wet and cold, Clementine climbs out of the well and up onto the porch. She watches them when they walk past windows. And the monsters. She watches them too. She isn't welcome here. They love to tell her that. They speak in unison, and their collective voices sound like so many hornets.

"Go away, Child of Light."

But Clementine wants to be nearer the boy, to tell him help is coming. She steps inside and is at once surrounded by demons, intent on suffocating her before the boy can feel even a wisp of hope.

The boy sits in a room upstairs, alone. The man busies himself downstairs. Clementine walks past the man, unwilling or maybe unable to affect him anymore, and finds the boy. He lies on his side, his eyes on the trees blowing in the wind outside his window while a TV show screams canned applause. Clementine sits on the floor—dirty and neglected like the rest of the house—and reaches up to him.

"Help is coming," Clementine whispers to the boy.

"Faith is the strength by which a shattered world shall emerge into light."
~ Helen Keller

Chapter 13

Just as we reach Butler, Nana's cell phone rings. Papa Da fell down and was taken to the hospital. We head straight there.

When we get to the emergency room, he's already inside somewhere, being seen. The boys and I sit down in the waiting room while my parents and grandmother find out what's going on.

"Don't you know that kid?" Shea says to me.

I look up from my phone. I was trying to respond to a text from Morgan. Now that Pearl has a date, Morgan doesn't want to go out to dinner just the two of us. She's afraid it'll make people think we're lesbians.

"Who?" I ask.

There, on the other side of the waiting room, sits Hayden.

"You know him, right?"

"Yeah," I say.

"Well, aren't you going to say hi?"

By now, Shea, always the irksome child, is saying hi for me. He's waving happily across the room at Hayden, who now feels obliged to mosey over.

"What are you doing here, Gracie?" Hayden asks, like the ER waiting room is some kind of elite party, and I didn't get an invitation, so I must be crashing.

"Our Papa Da fell down," Sean tells him.

"Pa-pa-da?" Hayden repeats, finding the name hilarious.

"What are you doing here?" I ask.

He lifts his right hand and shows us his middle finger, which is covered in a bloody paper towel. "Chopping wood," he says.

We all nod.

"Gross," Sean says.

"Um, and you're still sitting in the waiting room?" Shea asks as we watch blood drip from the paper towel to the tile floor.

"Are you here by yourself?" I ask. Why would anybody send a teenager all alone to the emergency room with a bloody finger? And how did he get here? Our neighborhood is five miles from the hospital. Did he drive here?

Hayden looks at me then, and there's something about the glint of his eyes, or maybe it's something that happens to his face, and suddenly, I almost cry. I blink, confused. What's making me upset? Am I totally nuts? But he looks so alone, so . . . unloved, or something like that.

Thankfully, the nurse calls his name, and Hayden leaves.

"Thanks a lot," I say to Shea.

"What? I think he likes you, Gracie." He winks at me. I sigh and glance up to see Hayden's back before he disappears around the corner. Does he? And if he does, do I care?

Mom and Dad walk through the double doors that go back to the emergency room, carefully guiding Papa Da between the two of them. Nana pulls up the rear, carrying stuff. I stand up when I see them coming.

"Taw may guh hyun-tock!" Papa Da says, and he sounds jolly enough, so I assume this is some kind of reassurance on his part.

"Broken toe, that's all," Dad says.

By now, Shea and Sean have joined me, and we head out the door. A man holding an overnight bag in one hand and guiding a very pregnant-looking woman with the other walk up the sidewalk as we leave, so I hold the door for them. As they pass me, for five seconds or so I clearly see, I mean *clearly*, an entirely white figure with enormous wings walking behind her. I stand there and watch them. I can't stop looking. I realize I'm frozen. For a second, I can't speak. Clearly, nobody else sees the angel. By now, my family is half way to the car.

"Gracie!" Mom calls.

I watch the image dissolve. She's there, kind of following the pregnant lady, and then she fades into air. I close my eyes and open them. Gone. But I know what I saw. And all at once, I know the baby that this lady is about to deliver is in distress right now—inside his mom's tummy—but he'll be okay, and so will she. And I know he's a boy too. How do I know these things? And why?

I run back inside the hospital and down the hall to the maternity wing.

"Hey," I say.

The angel is gone. But the husband and wife are standing in front of a table. I guess they're checking in.

"You're going to have a boy, and he's going to be fine." I'm out of breath from running so fast.

The couple, and the nurses as well, look at me like I'm crazy, so I back away.

"Everything is going to be okay," I say, and the angel appears again, right there in front of me. It's like one of those movie dissolves. I watch her fade into the scene. She reminds me of my white-haired lady. Their faces are different, and this one is bigger, but they have the same translucent quality, like if I touched her, my finger would slide through her. This lady looks older, though. Is my white-haired lady an angel? Is she *my* angel?

I make my way back to the car.

Tonight's the Homecoming Dance. Morgan comes to my house for dinner, which is fine. We make ourselves pasta and set the table with all our fanciest stuff. Meanwhile, World War III is unfolding upstairs in my bedroom. Apparently, the last time Bridget borrowed the dress that Mary was planning to wear tonight, *somebody* burned a hole in it, more or less right on Mary's right breast. It looks awful. They're upstairs whisper-screaming about it. I know they're whisper-screaming because I had the misfortune to walk in there a couple of times to grab my own stuff to get ready myself. They're not giving full voice to their rage because Mom and Dad will want to know who was smoking and how someone's cigarette found its way to my sister's breast. I'm wondering that myself. Mary was already in a foul mood because she thinks a girl from West Friendship High School, one of our rivals, deliberately tripped her at the meet. And now she doesn't have a dress. And I don't think she's too thrilled with her date, either. He's one of Tommy's friends, and Mary only met him a couple of times. And Mary thinks he's shorter than her.

Eventually, Mary finds another dress to wear, and she and Bridget come downstairs, both looking gorgeous. Bridget is wearing a black dress with a really snug fit. But Bridget's tall and slim, and she looks great. Plus, she pulled back the front part of her hair with combs and the rest of it is flowing all long and curly. Mary has on a dark red dress with a really pretty chiffon skirt and a halter top. People say redheads can't wear red, but this shade of red looks elegant on Mary, and she has all her long red hair in a loose bun with lots of curly tendrils hanging out. Amazingly, when the boys arrive, everybody seems pretty chummy. Mom takes pictures of all of us, my sisters with their cute dates, and Morgan and me with each other. I really loved my dress when Mom and I bought it. It's a light shade of peach, and it reminded me in the store of a dress from the 1920s. It has pretty beading all over the front, and I'm wearing white tights and flats so I don't have to worry about not being able to walk. We found a headband that has almost exactly the same beading as the dress. Morgan's dress is actually my favorite. It's an olive green color, which is one of my top favorite colors, especially on Morgan with her dark brown hair. It's form-fitting on top but has layers of loose-fitting skirt material on the bottom, so it would be really fun to dance in.

I almost put my arm around Morgan the same way Tommy and his friend have their arms draped around my sisters, just to be funny, but I think better of it. I don't think she'd laugh, not when she's already worried about our reputations as heterosexuals.

Dad is driving Morgan and me to the Homecoming Dance, and Tommy is driving my sisters. Tommy's friend doesn't impress me much. He didn't bring a corsage for Mary, and I watch him get into Tommy's car first instead of helping Mary. Maybe Caleb has a girlfriend, and maybe nobody likes me now, but someday I'm going to find a boy who will really like me and makes me feel important. And he'll hold the door for me too.

There are some things Grace O'Shaunessy just should not do. One thing, obviously, is to become a professional orator of tongue twisters. And a second is go to dances. Here I am at the second dance I've been to in my whole life, and I am again having a terrible time. First of all, it's ridiculously dark in the gym. The decorating committee spent *hours* hanging little stars all over the gym, and I can't see a single one. Actually, that's not totally true. There's this black-light strobe light thing flashing around intermittently, and so every once in a while I do see little cut-out silver stars swinging about. But they just make me think of the flashlights in Noah's neighborhood, reflecting back a lot of darkness.

I thought we had grinding at the eighth-grade dance, but it was nothing compared to this. I'm hoping I won't see my sisters because if they're dancing like this, I'll be mortified. I do see Marty and Lisa. They appear to be having virtual sex in the middle of the dance floor. Pearl and Scott come running over to Morgan and me. She introduces him to us. We have to scream over the music to be heard.

"Let's go outside!" Pearl yells.

"Okay," Morgan and I say, and all four of us go out to the hall. She introduces Scott to us again. Morgan acts like she's never seen him before. I think he seems nice.

"Hey, Grace!" I turn and see Caleb. He's with the girl I saw at the cross-country meet. They're holding hands.

"Hey!" I say, smiling broadly and trying to keep my eyes trained on his face and not his hand in hers.

"This is Cecile," he says. "She's French."

We all nod and smile at her. "Bonjour," says Pearl.

"Bonsoir," Morgan says, correcting Pearl, probably still mad. "It's nighttime."

"Tiens," Cecile says.

I can't think of a single thing to say. I wrack my brain, but I just can't.

After an awkward pause, Caleb says "Well, have fun." And he and Cecile step into the gym.

"Let's go up to the cafeteria," I say, not wanting to follow Caleb and his exotic girlfriend into the dance.

There's an enormous crowd upstairs. It strikes me as a bit ironic that everyone worked so hard to decorate the gym, got this really cool deejay, got dressed up in these expensive clothes, and went to fancy restaurants, just so we could all sit around in our good ol' school cafeteria with its fluorescent lights, consuming pretzels and warm coke. Maybe I could start a campaign to bring back dancing at dances. Maybe then more kids would be in the gym.

After a while, the four of us go back downstairs to the gym. I run into Hayden, or, more specifically, his finger. I mean, really, I run right into it.

He serenades me with expletives as I step away.

"Sorry! I didn't see . . . sorry."

"It's okay."

He looks nice. He has on a blue button-down and one of those really flashy Jerry Garcia ties.

"Date?" he asks. "I thought you had a date, Gracie."

"No." We stand there looking at each other. Hayden doesn't look like he's thinking about going anywhere else. "You?" I ask.

"No." At that moment, as luck would have it, the deejay plays a slow song.

"Dance?" Hayden asks.

"Okay."

It's an absolutely perfect four minutes. He smells nice—not too "axe-y"—and holds me just tight enough to make me feel . . . safe. We don't talk, but at one point he pulls away a bit and smiles at me. Then he thanks me, bows in this funny way, and disappears into the crowd. I start breathing again, and go looking for Morgan.

Finally, it's eleven o'clock, and we can go home. I never saw Caleb again after that one time, or Morgan, either. I think she left me. I mean, I think she went home without me. I saw Bridget and Tommy—they weren't grinding. They were just madly kissing in the corner. I guess I know what happened to Mary's dress. I mean, I guess I can figure out how the burn marks got there. I just didn't know Tommy smoked.

But Mary and her date have disappeared. I get my coat, and see, under a bunch of other coats, that Mary's coat is still here. She has this tacky zebra-patterned jacket, and she's definitely the only girl at our school with that coat. Grabbing both our coats, I go looking for her.

"Bridget!" I say, as I see Bridget and Tommy in the hall, already putting on their coats. "Where's Mary? I have her coat."

Bridget looks confused. With a sea of about fifty kids in between us, I can see her looking around and saying something to Tommy, who then turns and heads down the hallway. Bridget reaches me, and the two of us go outside. We both pull out our phones, but she's faster, so I stand there, imagining worse things every second Mary doesn't answer her phone. Most kids are outside by now, laughing and saying goodbye to one another. Some are walking to their cars, and others are waiting for rides.

Tommy comes outside, shaking his head. I guess he didn't find them inside. He pulls out his phone, and calls his friend, whose name, I learn, is Marc. After four or five rings, we hear someone answer.

"Where'd you go?" Tommy asks. He listens, and says, "What are you doing there?" Tommy feels in his pockets. Now he walks away from us, looking angry. "You took my effing car?"

Bridget wrestles his phone from him. "Marc? Marc?" Bridget must be very aggravated by Marc's response because she says, "Just shut up, lowlife." And then, "Let me talk to my sister."

We all stand there for a minute. By now most kids have either left in their own cars, or been picked up by parents. It's cold and dark. I spot Dad as he pulls into the parking lot. I don't think he sees us yet. Bridget and Tommy see him too. We all three of us move away from the streetlight so Dad won't spot us quite so soon.

"Gracie, you go," Tommy says, taking my shoulder, and he directs me, or actually more like shoves me, toward my father's car. I'm sure he's imagining the scene if my father finds out this guy went off somewhere with Mary, without her permission, in Tommy's car. Then, Bridget's talking to Mary.

"So come back now. How far away are you?" She closes her eyes and lets out a very agitated breath. "We're stranded here, Mary." Bridget pauses, listening. "Put him back on. Mary, put Marc back on." Bridget glares at Tommy.

"Gracie, go," Tommy repeats. My dad gets out of the car. Now he sees us.

"Hey, Marc," Bridget says, her back to the parking lot, ignorant that Dad is within earshot. "You do anything to my sister, I'll call the cops so fast you'll wish—"

"Hi, Mr. O'Shaunessy! How are you?" Tommy screams. I guess he hopes that if he's loud enough, Dad won't hear Bridget. Some chance.

Bridget stops talking and turns to Dad.

"What's going on?" Dad asks, looking at each of us.

For a moment, we all wait for someone else to say something. Then Bridget says, "Tommy's friend and Mary went to the Cow to get ice cream and left us stranded." Then she speaks into her phone, "But they're on their way back now."

"Yeah?" Dad says. My dad's no dummy. "Well, Gracie and I will wait to make sure everyone has a ride. Why don't you and Tommy join us while we wait?"

We follow him.

About ten long minutes later, Tommy's car pulls up. Dad opens his door first, before any of the rest of us even think to make a move. My dad has quick reflexes. He opens Tommy's passenger door and escorts my sister out of the car. Then he sits down in the car with Marc and closes the door behind him. Mary gets into the minivan. She looks upset, but she's not crying, at least not yet. She climbs into the backseat by herself, throws her head back, and closes her eyes. Bridget and I climb back there with her. Nobody says anything. We just sit there, waiting for her to come back from wherever she went, inside herself.

Finally, she opens her eyes, shakes her head, and says, "It's okay, you guys. I'm still a virgin." She laughs a shaky laugh. "He's...he's just a jackass."

She looks like she's going to start crying then, but Tommy says, "Actually, his last name is Âne, which does mean jackass in French." We all laugh at that, even Mary.

94

Dad gets back in our car and instructs Tommy to take his friend home, and to kindly not bring this boy around again. Tommy doesn't even try to say goodnight to Bridget. He just leaves.

Bridget and I stay on either side of Mary all the way home.

So goes my freshman Homecoming Dance.

"These things I warmly wish for you: someone to love, some work to do, a bit o' sun, a bit o' cheer, and a guardian angel always near."
~ Irish blessing

Chapter 14

This Sunday we all go to church. That's not typical at our house. Mom always goes because she teaches Sunday School, but for the rest of us, it's hit or miss. Maybe one week I'll go with Nana and Papa Da, or maybe all us girls will go, but we don't usually—all nine of us, or ten, if Peter's home—barrel into the minivan and go to church, like the Waltons or something. I can remember when I was a little girl, and we all went to church as a family, every Sunday. It was part of the weekly routine. That was back when my Pop-Pop was alive, Nana's husband. But if there's one thing I've learned about life, it's that I can't "freeze-frame" it. Every day something's different—sometimes the differences are so small, they sneak past me. But nothing stays the same. I'm looking at Sean sitting next to me in the car. For the first ten years of his life, I never—I mean *never*, even in pictures—saw that boy without an action figure in his hand. He and Noah used to spend hours acting out adventures with their guys. Now he barely touches them. He plays XBox all the time and talks about sports cars and cheat codes. He hasn't had a single light saber battle since Noah disappeared.

Even Mom has changed. She used to wear her hair loose and curly all the time, sporting dangly earrings and colorful skirts. She used to laugh more. She didn't used to worry as much. Or maybe I just wasn't tuned in.

We go to a small Episcopal church—Saint Paul's. Our sanctuary is probably at least one hundred and fifty years old. It definitely pre-dates the Civil War because it's on the walking tour we have in our town every summer when we observe the anniversary of Pickett's Charge.

Our family takes up two rows today. I guess everybody has stuff they want to pray for. I imagine what we all must sound like to God. Maybe we sound like a bunch of voices whispering up to some heavenly realm, like in *It's a Wonderful Life* when George Bailey is going to kill himself. I can almost hear this gigantic assortment of voices, old and young, boys and girls, all petitioning God at the same time. It blows my mind, thinking about how He could hear each one of us—and sort out needs from wants.

Sometimes when we sing, especially on the Sundays we sing more contemporary songs, I close my eyes and lift my arms to worship. Our church isn't very born-again, and most people don't do that. If my brothers or sisters are sitting near me, they grab me and pin my arms to my sides.

"Cut it out," one will whisper while the other elbows me in the ribs. But I get lost in worship sometimes. I paint pictures in my head, and they kind of pull me right out of the pew. Then, invariably, I have Bridget or Shea dragging me down.

Today, an elderly man who I see in church all the time, Mr. Bingham I think, is raising his arms and loudly singing—smiling and lifting his face to Heaven. He has to be eighty—maybe older. He's sitting next to a lady—she's in her eighties too. They look so contented. He's a widower. I remember when his wife died. I think she had cancer and was wheelchair-bound the last few months before she passed away. I'm glad he has a friend now to go with to church. I want to be like him when I'm old—I want to be able to lose myself in worship and sing loud and not care if I'm off-key. I'm sitting across the aisle from them, smiling about it. Bridget pokes me.

"What are you looking at, Gracie?"

I just shrug.

After church, Mary seems to be in a better mood. She and Mom go for a long walk. I see them from the window by my bed, where I'm now sequestered with my homework. I have to read two acts of *Hamlet*, journal for the play, and write a persuasive speech. It seems insensitive of teachers to assign homework over homecoming weekend. Then again, maybe if I'd kept up with what I was supposed to be doing, I'd feel less overwhelmed now.

Mr. Bowen is going somewhere! He has a couple of suitcases under his arms and something in a garment bag. I put down *Hamlet* and watch him put his stuff in the trunk.

"Where are you going?" I whisper to the room at large, pressing my nose against the screen. It's really pretty out today, so we opened all our windows to fill the house with fresh air. He hasn't left the house, at least when I've been home, in weeks.

I try to read. Hamlet's "To be or not to be" speech makes me think about whether or not I should go across the street right now or wait a little bit before I dig into my neighbor's wrapped-up Christmas presents.

"To unwrap or not to unwrap." I'm reading in my head. His car pulls out. I stay put for a minute, but the urge is too great. Still in my Sunday best, which is really just a skirt and sweater, I bolt.

I hear my brothers' voices in the basement.

"Invite me to your party!" Shea is yelling, or something like that. I really don't understand Xbox. I try to play sometimes. I'm awful. But I do know it's not a real party he wants to attend.

I walk out the back door. Our house is on a hill, and we have a stone path down to the road from the back door. All along the path are trees and bushes. We've got loads of enormous old trees in our neighborhood, too, and the Dunne's and Mr. Bowen's houses back up to really dense woods, so it's not hard to get around without being seen, at least before winter. I run fast and feel pretty sure nobody sees me. I head straight to the same basement window that was open the last time I was poking around here. Still unlocked. I crawl into the window well, thankful for once I'm so short, and push the window all the way open. Then I slide into the dark basement, feet first, and land on the floor. Easy. It's a sunny day, so it's not hard to see down here, even without turning on any lights. I walk to his huge pile of presents, lean over, and pick one up.

I unwrap it, fast. Ski goggles. He's giving somebody ski goggles—nice ones too. I look further into the pile. I pull out a bigger parcel. This one looks like it could be a sled. I unwrap just the edges. I was right. It is. So maybe the priest was right. These are Christmas presents. There are some presents wrapped in the same kind of paper I found by the footbridge—plain red with candy canes. Could this be proof? I pick up a present so I can show the police how it matches the paper I found, but I'm wondering how I can prove I found the piece of paper somewhere else. And even if I can, so what? What I need is evidence Noah was here—*is* here. I kneel down in the middle of the presents and feel my way through a bunch of them to try to find the book bag. I unwrap corners, figuring I don't want to re-wrap all this stuff. After twenty minutes or so, I'm pretty sure his book bag isn't down here. So I go upstairs. This house is crazy tidy. I look in the living room, bedrooms, kitchen. It's laid out like the Dunnes'. But it's so excessively clean, it almost makes me feel like nobody even lives here, like it's a model home or something. I open the refrigerator. Even the refrigerator is spotless. He has milk, cheese, two eggs. That's it.

Outside the kitchen window, I see Mary and Mom on our street walking Sweetie. I take another look in Mr. Bowen's bedroom. I lean against the door and try to concentrate on what I'm looking at. It's a little trick of mine—kind of like when I look at the Federal Express logo. Sometimes I just have to look between the E and the X for a few seconds before the arrow pops out at me. Sometimes I see the arrow right away, but not always. So I stand and study the room. I don't think Noah was ever in this room. I don't feel him here. I don't feel anything here. It's like this whole house is some kind of paper cut-out house. Nobody lives here.

I go back downstairs and grab a chair so I can climb back up into the window well. Then I kick the chair away from the window so nothing looks different. Squirreling out, I let a couple of leaves fall onto the basement floor. Halfway across his lawn, I remember I didn't re-wrap the presents. My stomach does a tumblesault.

I spend the rest of the afternoon on homework, or at least I try. I keep imagining Mr. Bowen finding the opened presents and knowing I was in his house, and then coming across the street. Somehow, he'd be able to shimmy up the tree outside my window and climb in, and laugh while he strangled me or something.

Monday on the bus, when Hayden says, "G-g-gracie", it sounds different somehow. There's something different about him. And Julie keeps staring at me. Finally, I ask her what's wrong.

"What were you doing in my neighbor's basement?" she asks.

I just look at her, speechless.

"I saw you climbing in," she says.

"He keeps an extra key for us, and I was locked out, of my house, I m-m-m-mean," I say, finally.

Hayden is interested. "Breaking into people's houses, G-G-Gracie?"

"He doesn't lock his basement window so we can—" I say. She doesn't believe me.

In public speaking class, it's my turn to give my persuasive speech. I found a video on the internet, and I use it as my attention getter. The kids all laugh—I was afraid of this, but I forge on.

"My goal is to persuade you that bumping and grinding isn't dancing, and that we should try to re-introduce the art of dancing to the high school dance." My classmates, especially the upperclassmen, are amused.

"Also, I'll try to explain what the actual act of grinding does physically to the teenage boy, and why it's a bad idea at a high school dance."

I want to talk about Mary's date, Marc Âne, and how worked up he got grinding with Mary, and how afterward, he almost raped her. But I couldn't betray her like that, so I skip that part.

It's a hard speech to give, and I stutter a lot. But I feel like most of the kids who were smirking in the beginning are taking me seriously at the end. I actually get pretty authentic-sounding applause. During discussion, Leo tells me he's impressed by me and my boldness, especially since I'm just a freshman. "Bold," he calls me. That's nice. I'd love to think I'm bold. Some other kids dismiss me as either a prude or a child, but I spoke what I felt. I was afraid they'd laugh at me, but I still did it. And that's progress for me.

Morgan's at rehearsal today, helping to paint the set. When I'm not on stage, I work with her, trying to make the walls of the garden house look like woodwork. Now that homecoming is over, she seems a lot more relaxed—about Pearl and Scott, and herself. Boys. Who needs them? We laugh about it. I almost tell her how upset I was that Caleb has a girlfriend. But I stop myself. It's not that I don't trust Morgan. It's just that, if I don't speak it, maybe it's not real.

We walk home together after rehearsal. She's going to have dinner with us. We talk about boys and how hard it is to be ourselves with them. Glad to be with my friend, I let my guard down.

"I don't trust the guy who lives across the street from us. I think he had something to do with Noah Dunne disappearing."

"Why do you think that?" she asks. Well, isn't that the million-dollar question?

"I just get a bad vibe. He's weird. He goes away to some other place, I think, and I don't think he even really lives in his house—I mean, you know, like, eats there or does laundry. I think his house is just a front—"

"A front for what?"

"Like, to make people think he's living a normal life."

"Grace?"

"I mean . . . For a couple of weeks, he *never* left. I mean, I'm not even exaggerating. He didn't go to work. He didn't even go inside. He hung out on his lawn, watering his brown grass and stuff, like he was teasing me, like he was telling me, 'Just try to see what I've got in here'. It was crazy, Morgan. And I'd walk by, and he'd be just looking at me."

"I think you're obsessed."

So now I'm sorry I told Morgan. Every time I talk about it, my thoughts get jumbled up. It's like my ideas are the straight edges of a thousand-piece puzzle, carefully laid out on a table, but giving voice to them is like somebody picking the table up in the air and throwing it against the wall.

"Probably," I say. And then we talk about whether or not we're too old to go trick or treating next week.

"This is how it will be at the end of the age. The angels will come and separate the wicked from the righteous."
~ Matthew 13:49

Chapter 15

Today is October 31st. Lots of kids come to school in costumes because it's Halloween. We're not supposed to. Unlike elementary school, where everybody dresses up, including my mother, or even middle school, where they at least have a festive pumpkin-carving competition between the grades, at Butler High School, today is business as usual. Getting dressed up every day during Homecoming Week is an anomaly—otherwise, we're not allowed to wear hats or even head scarves, never mind costumes. So today, lots of kids are getting discipline referrals. In English, one boy walks in dressed like the Statue of Liberty. My teacher sends him right back out the door. By the end of the day, the time-out room is full to the brim, and most of the teaching staff is in a pretty rotten mood.

At rehearsal, tension is high too. The show is next week, and today we're not allowed to call line anymore. That's not a problem for me—I only have one line. But Lisa, Leo, and Caroline are desperate to cram their lines into their heads. They're madly cueing each other backstage. Zach has known all his lines for about a month. I deposit the thought that if ever I get a part with lines, I want to be like Zach.

After rehearsal, I find my sisters, and we head home with Becca. As we drive through town, I see lots of little kids already running along sidewalks with their parents, decked out in costumes and sporting glow bracelets and plastic pumpkins.

When we get home, Shea is arguing with Mom about what he wants to wear tonight. Mom hates gruesome costumes. Her big argument against them is their corruption of little kids. So they're going at it in the front hall, with Shea in his Killer Clown costume—minus the ghoulish mask—and Mom with her ceramic party platter of Hershey chocolate.

"When did you even get that?" she's asking.

"Dad was with me. Dad paid for it. What do you want me to be, Mom? Thomas the Tank Engine?"

"Did you say this costume was okay?" Mom calls to Dad. Uh-oh. Now Shea has the parents duking it out. Never a good thing.

"What?" Dad says from the kitchen. I think he pretends he can't hear sometimes to give himself time to come up with an excuse. There's a knock at the door.

"Trick or treat!" I hear little kid voices sing out. I jump up to peek at them as Mom offers candy. And there stand kindergarten versions of Freddy Krueger, Jason in his hockey mask, and the Grim Reaper. So much for corruption. We all laugh, even Mom.

Papa Da is having dinner with us. I think Nana thinks he'll enjoy seeing the kids trick-or-treat. She starts talking about growing up in Brooklyn, and how she and her brothers and sisters would dress up and go knocking on people's doors looking for treats on Thanksgiving.

"Really?" I ask.

"Absolutely," she says. "We would cover our faces with dirt, or maybe coal, and I would wear my older sister's clothes that were too big for me, or maybe my mother's high heels, and we would go door to door, asking if there was anything for Thanksgiving."

"Weird," Shea says.

"Did you get candy?" asks Sean.

Papa Da shakes his head. He's enjoying this talk. He loves it when we talk about the past.

"I don't think so," Nana says, looking like she's trying to remember. "I think we usually got a piece of fruit or a few nuts."

Shea thinks that's hilarious. "Nuts?" he says. Then he shakes his head, chuckles some more, and when the next group of kids knocks on the door, he tries tossing walnuts into their plastic pumpkins. Mom shoves him out of her way just in time.

After dinner, I go outside with Shea and Sean. I'm not wearing a costume. Instead, I'm wearing this ski cap I got when I was in sixth grade. It's brown with bear ears sticking up on top and a bear's smiling face on the front. But my brothers are being children in Halloween costumes for one more year. I'm glad for that. Mom didn't want any of us to go out at all, not until Noah comes home. Dad won that fight, though. I'm surprised, actually. I heard them in the kitchen last night before dinner. Dad was saying that Americans couldn't refuse to ever fly again after September 11th, and Mom was telling him that argument did not apply to this situation *whatsoever*. She said that word really loud, repeatedly. Regardless, Dad prevailed, because here we three are, collecting candy.

Against my better judgment, and mainly because Shea insists Mr. Bowen gives out huge chocolate bars, we knock on his door. He opens the door and acts like he's delighted to see us. He talks about how tall we're all getting and directs us not to finish all our candy before we get home. I wonder in passing if he laced it with arsenic. My eyes wander behind him as he's leaning over to collect our bags of goodies. In the corner of the living room, behind an armchair, is a book bag with a picture of Darth Maul on it. My eyes are glued to it. It's Noah's. I totally know it because Noah and Shea had a big argument about it before school started. Shea told him he'd look dorky with a Star Wars book bag in middle school. And Noah told Shea he didn't care. I can almost hear them talking. They were on our front lawn. Noah and Sean were just back from bike riding, and Shea was just being nasty. Or maybe he thought he was protecting Noah.

By now my brothers have gotten their treats and said thanks. I guess they didn't look inside the house.

"Gracie," Shea says, probably wondering why I'm lingering. I look at Mr. Bowen, swallow slowly, and open my pillowcase for some poisoned candy.

"Happy Halloween," my brothers say, already running down his porch steps.

"Can I use your bathroom?" I ask.

Mr. Bowen looks at me, and if he doesn't want me to come in, he covers really well.

"Sure," he says, while the boys turn around, confused.

"Gracie, what are you doing?" says Sean.

"Our house is across the street. Use our bathroom," says Shea.

My mind is racing. How can I take that bag? I study it with my eyes, without turning my head, as I walk to his bathroom, which is in the opposite direction. He starts to tell me where the bathroom is, and then stops when he sees I know where I'm going.

"Your house is just like the Dunnes'," I say, probably explaining too fast. He screws up his eyebrows a little bit.

I go into the bathroom and lock the door behind me. What am I doing? I look at myself in the mirror. I see myself in the mirror, looking kind of crazy in my teddy bear ski cap, and I see shadows surrounding me. I turn around fast. There's nothing here. I guess I'm losing it. But I smell something too — that same sulfur smell that was in the woods, that's in my dreams. Any second now, I'll be humming my motor noise and then everybody will know Gracie has officially cracked.

I put down the toilet lid and sit, thinking about ways I can get the bag. I realize I have to divert Mr. Bowen's attention. I could grab it and run. That seems risky. I could call him. I grab my phone out of my coat pocket. He'd have to leave the room to get the phone. But what's his number?

"Gracie!! What are you doing?" Shea yells. They're outside. I see my brothers through the bathroom window.

I could take a picture of the book bag. I have a camera on my phone. My hands sweaty and shaking, I pull my phone out. I'll act like I'm just holding it and push the button as I walk by. And he could grab me, my phone, and both my brothers, and do to us whatever he did to Noah. Then my mother will die of a nervous breakdown.

I think about Hamlet, standing around doing nothing but spouting monologues, and Helen, acting — even when she had no idea what was literally in front of her face. I unlock the door and hide my phone behind my pillowcase, with my shaking fingers ready to snap a picture as I pass the chair. I walk into the living room. Mr. Bowen is on the front porch, chatting amiably with Shea and Sean.

And the book bag is gone. It's gone. I stop and look at the place where it was. I look out the front door. Mr. Bowen glances back at me.

"Everything okay, hon?" he asks, sounding normal.

I nod. No words come out. He knows. He knows I know what he did.

I walk out the front door, fast. The boys follow me, waving again and wishing him a Happy Halloween. Once past his fence, I look back. He's still on his porch. He waves at me. Smooth. Smooth-talking kidnapper.

"It's late," I say. "Let's go home." We're standing on the corner. I'm sure he's still watching us. I have to keep acting normal.

"Not yet, Gracie," Sean says. "Let's go down Oak Drive."

I shake my head. "Mom wants us home. She just texted me," I lie.

So we cross the street and climb up the hill to our house. I head straight to the family room. Mom is hunkered over her sketch pad, drawing something with lots of dots, and everybody else is watching a *Seinfeld* rerun.

"Noah's book bag was in Mr. Bowen's living room," I blurt out. "We have to call the police."

Sean and Shea, moments ago stuffing their faces with Kit Kat bars, look baffled.

On TV, George Costanza is explaining to Jerry how easy it is to lie if you believe it when you say it.

Bridget mutes the sound.

"No, it wasn't," Shea says.

"Where'd you see it?" Sean asks.

"He hid it after he knew I saw it." My voice sounds all warbly, like a guitar string tuned too high. Mom stands up.

"What?" Mom asks. "Baby, what are you talking about?"

"Are you on drugs?" Bridget asks.

"Bridget!" Mom says.

Dad comes downstairs.

"I saw Noah's Darth Maul book bag. It was sitting on the floor. So I went in the bathroom and got out my camera. But then he . . ."

"What?" asks Dad. If one more person in this family says 'what', I'll lose it. "We're wasting time," I hear myself screaming. "He's hiding it. Let's call the police!" I pull out my cell phone.

"Wait!" Dad says. "Wait! Gracie, calm down. What the *hell* are you talking about?"

The thought crosses my mind that everybody is in on this, that Mr. Bowen has infected them all, maybe replaced my family, friends, the local priest with some kind of *Stepford Wives* people.

"Noah's book bag, Dad. With Dark Maul on it—you know the bad guy with the red face and the yellow—"

"Right. Right. And?"

"Well, why do *you* think Noah's book bag is in Mr. Bowen's house, Dad?"

"I don't," he says. Dad's expression is a combination of confusion and irritation. He looks pissed off, in fact.

"Well, why would . . . what would he . . . he's a grown man, Dad. Why would he have a kid's book bag?"

"Gracie. The police have looked in every nook and cranny of that man's house."

"What?" This is news to me.

"They *combed* his house. He was glad they did. He wanted them to."

"Dad, what do you m—?"

He cuts me off. "He's a single guy. He's living alone." Dad pauses, like maybe he doesn't want to say anything else. He looks at my brothers, my mom. By now everybody's standing up, watching my dad, waiting.

"So?" asks Shea.

"Jason Bowen was falsely accused before. Okay? His world was turned upside down."

I'm still not getting it. "What?"

"His wife left him. She got a restraining order so he couldn't see his son. He lost his job. Then, after all that . . . crap . . . he was found innocent."

"When was this?" Mary asks.

"Innocent of what?" Bridget asks.

"But once you're falsely accused, your character is always suspect."

"Falsely accused of *what*, Dad? Murder?" Shea asks.

Dad looks at Shea. "Molestation."

Nobody says anything.

"So when Noah disappeared, Bowen immediately presented himself to the police. Gracie, they searched every inch of his house. He's clean."

Certainty crawls across every nerve of my body. Mr. Bowen did it. He took Noah. He molested him like he did his own son. He did something once, and he's done something again.

"Taw may tin," Papa Da says. I forgot he was here. He's sitting by himself in the corner of the family room.

"How was he found innocent?" Mom asks Dad. So she didn't know about all this stuff, either.

"Because she dropped the charges, Mae. She admitted she made it up."

"Made it up?" Mom looks horrified.

"She was trying to hurt him."

"Where's his son now?" Mom asks. "I've never seen—"

"Dead."

"Dead?" Shea and Mom say, almost at once.

"How did he die?" Bridget asks.

"Suicide."

Says who? I think to myself. Nobody talks for a little bit. Finally, I say, still holding my phone, "But Dad, why would he have a kid's book bag? And why did he hide it?"

"Hide it?"

"I . . . used his bathroom, and when I came out, it was gone. He put it away somewhere."

"Why were you using his bathroom? You could come home and use your own bathroom."

"Dad, did you hear what I just said? *He hid it.* Why would he do that?"

"Gracie O'Shaunessy, listen to me. I don't know why Jason Bowen likes *Star Wars* book bags. I don't know why your mother carries all her art supplies in a *Ninja Turtles* book bag, either. Here's what I do know. *You* need to leave this man alone."

My dilemma is that I'm generally an obedient kid. I absolutely disagree with Dad, and I know I need to go to the police, and I know Dad's been duped. But he's my dad. And he told me not to. So it's what you'd call a stalemate. I just stand there.

The family kind of disperses after that. Finally, it's just me and Papa Da.

"Coll-een mott," he says.

"Air-inn go braw, Papa Da," I tell him, the only Irish I know.

I don't call the police. I guess that gives Bowen plenty of time to hide Noah's book bag—or destroy it.

***

Bowen is scared. He's scared of Grace. Clementine follows him to the mountains and watches him drop the bag into the well.

She finds the boy and encourages him. If she can build up his armor, he can fight.

"I am not afraid of storms for I am learning how to sail my ship."
~ Helen Keller

Chapter 16

Noah's 5K is a total success. We hold it the first Saturday of November, and it's 60 degrees with just a tiny breeze and not a cloud in the sky. It's like God gave us this totally unexpected weather to do this thing. Loads of people participate. We hold it at the Butler City Playground. The cross-country team charted out an excellent course and marked it with banners and chalk. We have volunteers working as timers, and tee shirts with Mom's design on them. Everyone who's running is wearing a shirt. They're blue. Noah's parents picked the color, and they really liked the single candle. We have sponsors who donated food, drinks, ribbons, trophies. Our local radio station, WTJR, is here too. Not everybody is running—some are walking, and some aren't running or walking, but they're still donating. I'm hoping it makes Julie and her parents feel a little bit less alone. We charge a $5 entry fee. Dad and a couple of other parents are sitting at a registration tent, taking money and looking very official, writing everything down on their yellow legal pads.

I run and do pretty well, considering I'm not training like my sisters. Peter runs, too, and so do a bunch of his friends from St. Anthony's. Caleb runs. I don't see Cecile with him. I hope they broke up. Hayden runs, and that surprises me. I'm glad to see him. I notice that outer layer of thug is harder to see on him since he danced with me.

Afterward, Noah's dad stands up on the dais and thanks everybody for coming. WTJR set up microphones and speakers, but when Mr. Dunne starts to speak, everybody gets really quiet. I bet we would have heard him without any amplification.

"Thanks, everyone. Thanks to John and Mae O'Shaunessy for doing this, and their crew." He nods to us. "Thanks to all the sponsors and the kids who did so much work." He pauses and bows his head, and everyone gets even quieter. Mrs. Dunne walks up to him and holds his hand. Then Julie does too.

It makes me think of the vigil at their house. "We're very thankful. The money will go to helping us find our son."

When he says the word "son", he crumples. The priest, the first person to tell me to leave Mr. Bowen alone, leads us all in a prayer. While we're all bowing our heads for the prayer, I scan the crowd to see who else is here. Bowen is here. I didn't see him earlier. I'm pretty sure he missed the race part, and he doesn't have on a tee shirt. I think about how they say serial killers like to go to the funerals of their victims. Maybe that's what he's doing. Or maybe he's watching me while I'm watching him. He has on sunglasses, and he's looking in my direction, so he *could* actually be looking at me. Or maybe he's scanning the crowd for some other boy he can kidnap. The thought makes me nauseous.

Caleb and I literally bump into each other at the refreshment tent.

"Hey," I say.

"This is terrific," he says. For a second, I think he means his sandwich. Then I realize he's talking about the event. "Uncle Tim and Aunt Pat really appreciate it." I keep forgetting he's related to Julie.

"Where's your . . . friend?" I ask.

He looks confused.

"Cecile?" I add.

"Oh! I don't know." Then we both smile and nod.

"She's beautiful," I say, not having planned to say that. I don't want to talk about how pretty Cecile is, and certainly not to Caleb. She is, though. She has long, silky blonde hair and one of those elegant Parisian noses. She makes me look like a cocker spaniel puppy.

He's smiling at me and nodding. "She sure is," he says. I'm suddenly not sure if he's talking about Cecile or someone else, and I feel myself turning red.

"So where is she today? Not a runner?" Why on earth am I still talking about her?

"Who? Cecile?"

"Right."

112

"Somewhere." He laughs. "With friends, I guess. She has friends in the exchange program. They do a lot of stuff together."

"She's a foreign exchange student?"

"Yeah. Sure. She's my host sister. I told you that."

"No. You didn't. Isn't that . . . weird to be dating your . . . host sister?"

I say it before I can stop myself. Caleb looks surprised.

"I'm not . . . dating Cecile. What made you think I was?"

I just stand there looking at him, looking way up at him. Caleb is probably a foot taller than me.

"I . . . don't know, I just —" I feel like the sun just peeked out from behind a gigantic dark cloud.

Caleb laughs again.

At that moment, Mr. Bowen walks past us, smiles and nods at me, and as he does, jostles me a little bit.

"Sorry," he says.

I lose my train of thought.

"Grace?" Caleb asks. I look at him. "Are you okay?"

"Yeah," I say.

"What are you doing after the race?"

By now, Mr. Bowen has disappeared back into the crowd. My body is shaking.

"Grace? Hey, are you okay?"

I'd hate to throw up in front of Caleb, but I think I'm about to do just that.

"Sit down," he says. He leads me to a bench. "Maybe you ran too hard."

I cover my face with my hands and lean my elbows on my knees, and breathe. The feeling of bile in my throat subsides. Caleb must've gotten me water because when I sit up, he offers me a cup. I look for Mr. Bowen. He's gone.

Caleb hangs around for the rest of the race. He's helpful. By day's end, we've cleaned everything up and packed up tents, chairs, and equipment. As the sun sets, it cools off, and I'm wishing I was wearing more clothes. We raised a little over $8,000.00 for the Dunne family.

Tommy worked double-duty today. I think his intentions regarding Bridget are truly gentlemanly ones, and he seriously regrets displeasing Dad, not to mention Mary, with Marc Âne. It took Dad a while to warm up to Tommy. He's not an athlete, so they never had that safe subject as a buffer for neutral conversation. And he hasn't figured out any career path. He got into Towson, which is a good school, but I think—beyond college—Tommy's not too interested right now in where life will take him, which would be fine with Dad if Tommy wasn't dating Bridget. Dad wants to know where life is taking Bridget.

So today Tommy's been aiming to prove his worth, hauling tents and tarps and speakers. Caleb is a big help, too, but in Caleb's case, I think that's just the way he is.

Caleb and I elect to walk home when all the work is done, by ourselves. Mom loads us down with bags of leftover rolls, and we're off. We banter back and forth easily. He tells me all about what it's like to have a foreign exchange student staying with his family. He has a sister, Beth, who's a senior, and so is Cecile. The first month was terrific. Beth and Cecile got along famously. This second month, though, has had some drama. The girls bicker a lot, and Caleb's parents are fed up. Cecile is talking about moving in with a different host family.

"What are they fighting about?" I ask, thinking about my sisters and how things can get between them.

Caleb shrugs. "Anything, really. Clothes. Guys. Who said what, and why she said it. And there's this language barrier, you know? And our house wasn't so big to begin with, and now it seems a lot smaller."

We walk in silence while the sky turns orange. It's nice. I suggest we stop at the pond and feed the ducks with some of this extra bread. So we scale down a hill to the duck pond, holding on to each other to avoid falling, or maybe we just want a reason to make contact. Once we're on level ground, we don't let go.

"Cold?" Caleb asks. I nod, and he wraps his cross-country windbreaker around me. I get shivers all over, not the kind I get when I sense something bad. This is a different feeling, a new feeling. A nice feeling.

I'm thinking maybe I could talk to Caleb about the book bag and also my frustration that I can't get a single grownup to help me. I look up at him. He is so cute. He has honey-colored hair that's a cross between golden and brown, with gorgeous highlights reflecting off the setting sun. It's kind of shaggy, and kind of in between long and short, with a couple of messy banana curls that stick out willy-nilly. And he has dimples, really deep ones, that make him look like a little boy when he laughs. When I touch him, I mean when I brush up against him for any reason, the feelings I get are good—like sunshine or hearty laughter or bonfires on the beach. Warm. That's it. He makes me feel like I'm wrapped up in a blanket. He doesn't finish sentences for me, either, when I stutter. He just waits. I really like that about him.

"Have you ever felt like people don't hear you?" I say. "I mean, like they're speaking a different language, and you can't find the words to make them understand you?" I realize I'm fingerspelling beginnings of words as I try to explain what I mean. Nervous habit. So I stick my hands in my pockets.

"Sure. Why?" He offers what's left of his last roll to a couple of aggressive ducks.

"Well, I have a neighbor, and I don't like him . . . at all. And . . . I've been having bad feelings about him . . ."

Now I have Caleb's total attention. "Did he hurt you?"

"No! Me? No! But . . . well, I have a theory that this guy is involved in what happened to Noah."

"What do you mean . . . a theory?"

"I have this . . . I don't know . . . sixth sense or something . . . this . . . feeling that he's a bad person. And I've been inside his house a couple of times, and there's weird things about his house."

Caleb's not saying anything, but he doesn't look mad, so I keep going.

"He had a book bag that was the same one Noah had. I saw it on Halloween. And I told my father about it, and he got mad at me and told me

115

this guy is a good guy. And his house is so neat, I m-m-mean . . . like m-m-model home neat . . . like nobody lives there neat. And I just can't explain myself, but I think—"

"Tell the police. Talk to the police."

I'm relieved. He didn't tell me I was wrong, or crazy. "But they'll want real evidence. And the priest at your church *and* my dad both told me I was wrong to think all this. They both said Mr. Bowen has already been through hell and—"

"Bowen?" Caleb looks shocked.

"Oh, you know him?" I say.

"The guy who lives in your neighborhood?"

"Yeah."

"Yeah, I do. He goes to my church." Caleb pauses and shakes his head, like he's surprised, I guess. "He was my Cub Scout leader."

At first I don't say anything. But I'm so sick of this guy fooling everybody.

"So you think he's terrific, and I shouldn't think bad things about him, right?" I know my words sound mean, but I can't help it.

I toss the rest of my bread into the pond.

Caleb looks down and doesn't say anything. I climb up the hill, and he follows me. After a few quiet minutes, he says, "Sorry. I just know the story from church. He found his son's body after . . . he shot himself. I think he was our age. His son, I mean. Our age now. It happened a long time ago."

"Are you sure Mr. Bowen didn't shoot him?"

"Well . . . yeah. I mean, I guess so, right? They must've done an autopsy."

"Yeah, right."

Another closed door. That's how I feel, like I'm running down this crazy, long, winding hallway, and doors keep slamming.

"Hey," I add. "My dad said he wasn't allowed to *see* his son. He said that Mr. Bowen's wife had gotten a restraining order after she accused him of molesting him, so how could *he* have found his son dead?"

Caleb shrugs. We don't say anything for a bit. I ask him if he wants to run. We do. That warms me up, and I give Caleb back his jacket.

"Grace, I just know what I remember. My parents brought him food and stuff. I don't know why he has a kid's book bag, or about his house or anything. I just . . ."

"Right," I say.

Maybe Caleb thinks I'm wrong too. I can add his name to Mr. Bowen's fan club, but to his credit, he doesn't say anything else about it. It's hard to go back to carefree chatter, though. And I'm kind of mad at myself that I put a damper on things. We were having fun.

He walks me to my back door. I look across the street and see nobody's home at Mr. Bowen's house. Caleb follows my eye.

"See you at school?" he asks.

"See you at school," I say. He leans over and gives me a quick kiss. He misses my mouth, but that's okay. He takes off fast then, probably as embarrassed as I am.

I step inside. I just got my first actual kiss from a boy.

Mom is making dinner in the kitchen, and Bridget is filling water glasses at the window. I walk in, grinning, and Mom doesn't look up from the stove. Bridget turns to me, nods, and winks.

"Never bend your head. Always hold it high. Look the world straight in the eye."
~ Helen Keller

Chapter 17

I wake up, soaking wet. How can anybody sweat so much? Even my sheets are wet. I look across my room. Bridget and Mary are asleep. The assorted clocks say 2:14 a.m. I twist on a Christmas light—this one's yellow so now there's this golden hue to my whole corner of the room. Tomorrow—I mean today—is Monday, and the play's this week, so I should be asleep. I get up to put on a dry tee shirt, and once up, I figure I'll try to commit tonight's crazy dream to memory.

I step into the family room, red embers still glowing in the wood stove. It got crazy cold today, and felt even colder since it was so warm on Saturday. I grab a comforter off the couch and wrap it around myself. Then I sit on the floor, rest my head on my knees, and try to watch my dream, like a movie, in my head. I can feel it slipping away. So I get up and locate pen and paper. I try to draw it, but there's too many images cascading into each other. So I use words instead.

"I hear that sound, a ripping sound, like a huge bolt of fabric," I write, trying to describe the noise that's been scaring me awake all my life, "and I see the mist and shadows again, and the fingers. But this time it's different. This time I'm stronger, and I can control the floating. I can propel myself away from the things that scare me. So I do, and I kind of swim through the mist until it clears. And now my feet hit the ground, and I'm in an enormous field. There are flowers of every imaginable color. My mom would love this place. Wildflowers blow in a sweet breeze—it smells . . . heavenly. And then, in front of me, are these strips of muslin, huge strips, hanging from somewhere way high in the air, so high I can't see the top. They're blowing, too, like clothes on a clothesline. They're like a wall. I walk in between two strips, and in front of me are angels, but they're not grown-up angels, like the ones I see in church and on Christmas cards. They're children. And these angel children are playing with real children. They're spread out all over this

119

field of wildflowers. There must be hundreds, and they're laughing and running. I feel so happy just standing there. And then I recognize the white-haired lady, and I see she has wings, and that's she just a girl. She sees me, too, and runs to me. Then she stops, and all the children stop playing, and everybody looks past me, up high. I feel the darkness even before I turn around and see a huge dark shadow floating across the sky. It's colder. Grey fog is bleeding right through the muslin. And the colors of the flowers bleed to gray. And in the place where I just walked, right where the muslin was blowing like clean cotton sheets, sits Noah's book bag. There's no way it was there a moment ago. It just showed up. All the muslin is gone. I step closer to the bag and pick it up. Darth Maul's yellow eyes are looking at me. And it's heavy. And soaking wet. I know I should look inside, but I can't. I know what's inside is awful."

I put the pen down, and reread what I wrote. By now the fire is almost gone. I should go back to bed. I'm thinking that maybe I'll just sleep right here in front of the stove when I catch a glimpse of the night sky through the kitchen window. It's snowing. How crazy is that? Yesterday it was 60 degrees, and today it's snowing. Only in Maryland.

So using my blanket as a coat, I step into my boots and slip outside. There's a shimmery white coating of new snow on everything—tree branches, picnic table, a lone soccer ball, the stone steps down to the road. I look up to my window. My yellow Christmas light glistens in my window. Everywhere else, up and down the street, is pitch black. And quiet.

"Oh, God, what am I supposed to do? What should I do?" My voice sounds thin in the cold night air. I hope it weighs enough to float up to Heaven.

I stick my tongue out and taste the new snow, and then pull my blanket over my head and wrap myself up tighter. I scan the neighborhood—the houses, cars, the Dunnes' backyard, Mr. Bowen's fence. I look at the shed in Mr. Bowen's backyard. Shed? It's dark green and kind of blends in with the woods. It's on the far side of his yard. I never noticed it before. I never knew there was a shed back there. How come I've lived here almost my whole life, and I never saw that shed? I wonder if it's locked.

I step carefully down the path to the road. It's cold and icy out here. I use the yellow light shining from my window to guide my feet. I step into the road and almost fall on a patch of black ice. Then I run across to the Dunnes' yard and climb under Mr. Bowen's fence, getting my blanket and myself completely wet. I run to his shed. It's locked.

By now my hands are shaking, and I'm sure when I turn around Mr. Bowen will be running across the yard with a great big knife or something, like Norman Bates in *Psycho*. But I keep trying to pull the door open.

"Noah?" I say, trying to send my voice into the crack between the door and the wall. What if Mr. Bowen has been keeping him here in this shed, like Phillip Garrido did to Jaycee Dugard? What if Noah was here the whole time, drugged or something, or gagged?

"Noah? Noah?" I pull the door as hard as I can, hoping I'll break it. Instead, I fall down. I crawl back to the door and bang on it. "Noah!"

Noah's not here, Grace.

My body whips around, which makes me totally lose my footing and wind up sitting in the snow. Who said that? I look all around his yard, the woods. I'm alone. I can't stop panting, and my heart hurts.

It takes me a long time to work up the courage to move. I'm leaning against the shed wall, and I feel like as long as I don't move, at least nothing can creep up on me from behind. But once I start the long trek home, if someone is waiting to attack me in the woods, I'm an easy target. But it's cold. And I'm scared out here. So I move.

As I walk home, a car turns the corner. I'm ten feet from the road, and I collapse onto the wet ground and cover myself with my comforter, which is, by the way, *not* white, but a vivid patchwork of every fabric Mom has sewed in the last twenty years—my point being, I don't blend in.

But I try to stay still. I figure if I don't move, in the dark maybe I'll look like a mound of trash or something. I stay put until the car has passed. I hear it slowing down. I peek out and watch it turn left onto Evergreen Way, and pass the Dunnes', and pull into Mr. Bowen's driveway. I get up and run across the street, up the steps, and into our house. Once inside, I lock the door. By now I'm freezing, and the blanket is soaked. I look out the kitchen window. A light comes on in Mr. Bowen's living room. I see shadows moving through the curtains. I think I see a second person. Whoever it is, if there *is* a second person, he's a lot taller than Noah. But even so, even if it's not Noah, what's Mr. Bowen doing cavorting around in the middle of the night? And who's with him?

I grab the paper I wrote my dream on and run upstairs to my room. Once in bed, I unscrew the yellow bulb and perch elbows and chin on the windowsill, watching and waiting. Eventually, his living room light goes off. I guess they go to sleep. Finally, I do too.

In school, I've been working on a picture for the art show. I think we're going to display our work in the lobby outside the auditorium this weekend during the play. I was working on a sketch of Helen feeling water as it came out of the pump, trying to show the moment of connection, when Helen knows that the sound of the word, and the vibrations she feels, and the letters Annie fingerspells into her hand all mean the same thing—they all mean this *water* coming out of the pump. But it's been so hard. I kept erasing things— her eyebrows, her mouth, even her fingers as they strained to touch the drops of water. I just couldn't get it right.

So today I decided to try to capture the image I have in my head of the angel children playing with the real children in the field of wildflowers. They all looked so happy. This is proving just as hard. Every time I try to draw joy, it comes off looking like the kind of smile a child would make for a camera at *Sears*. So I erase it again.

I wish I could draw like my mom. I wish I could create nuances of rapture or amazement or delight with a paintbrush or pencil. Frustrated with myself, I stop and study the little boy's face that I drew. I drew Noah.

When my sisters and I arrive home, everybody's in the family room watching the news.

"Shhh," Dad says as we start asking what happened.

The newscaster is talking about a missing boy. His name is Jacob something, and he lives in Reisterstown, MD. That's not so far from us. He's fourteen years old and was last seen yesterday afternoon, walking home from a friend's house. A picture of him flashes up on the screen. It's a formal picture that a photographer took. His parents probably have the same picture framed on their wall.

I suck in breath and cover my mouth.

"What?" says Mary.

I'm sure this new boy, this Jacob, was the second person in Mr. Bowen's house last night. Bowen kidnapped him and brought him back to his lair. So where is Jacob now? Out in the shed with Noah? Dead?

"I saw Mr. Bowen come home in the m-m-m-m . . ."

"Middle? Are you trying to say 'middle'? Gracie?" Mary has that ticked-off voice she uses when I'm trying to tell her something, and it takes too long—which, of course, makes me stutter more.

"What are you, watching him in the middle of the night?" Bridget asks.

"Dad," I say, ignoring them, and focusing on him—the guy who could most likely drive me to the police station so we can report this, so we can save this Jacob kid. "It was two a.m. I couldn't sleep." I don't include the shed part. "I saw Mr. Bowen pull up with someone. I saw two people . . . through his curtains. I saw two shapes."

Mom and Dad are studying me. So is everyone else.

"Baby," Dad says, and as soon as I hear him speak, I know he's not driving me anywhere. "You think Jason Bowen kidnapped this boy from Reisterstown?"

I nod.

"Why, exactly?"

"I . . . just . . . think it makes sense. And he knows I know, Dad."

The newscast is over. Mom turns off the TV and starts telling all us kids she doesn't want us walking anywhere by ourselves. My sisters and Shea go upstairs.

Nana and Mom go to the kitchen. Sean doesn't move from his corner of the couch. I sit down next to him.

"Gracie, you've got to stop this," Dad says.

"Stop what?"

"Trying to save . . ." Dad stands up and walks away from us. "Noah. He's been gone for two months."

I imagine Helen, the way she was when she was a little girl—before Annie. I think about the scene in the early part of the play when I'm acting like such a brat, and I fully realize—in this moment, sitting here looking at Dad—that it's utter frustration that makes Helen such an obnoxious little girl. It's the rage you feel when you can't get anybody to understand you.

Dad goes into the kitchen, probably to whisper to Mom about how ol' Gracie has gone off the deep end. I look at Sean.

For a moment, he leans his head on my shoulder, and we hang that way for a bit, the kind of moment we used to have more often when he was little, and then he leaves too.

I go down to the basement and do laundry. I take stuff out of the dryer, load it with wet clothes, and fill the washing machine with assorted dirty clothes. The back part of our basement, where we keep our washer and dryer, is O'Shaunessy Memory Lane. First, there's all our Christmas stuff, which includes ornaments, lights, and handmade decorations that go back to Mom and Dad's newlywed days. Plus, we've got doll houses and dress-up trunks down here that my sisters and I used to play with for hours. We've got tricycles, buckets of Matchbox cars, Thomas the Tank Engine, and miles of track. Sean's collection of action figures has taken a back seat to Xbox recently, and so all his little guys are here too. I sort through them and notice he's got two of everything. He probably has all Noah's guys here too. The last time they played with them was this past summer.

I crouch down on the cement floor and set up Obi-wan Kenobi to battle General Grievous, and then I put Padmé on the sidelines with her arms up in the air. I sift through superheroes and villains, and finally find an Anakin. Then I set him up to help Obi-wan battle the bad guy.

"Gracie? Are you downstairs?" Mom calls.

"Yes!"

"Dinner!"

I stand up with the basket of folded clothes, leaving the good guys poised to beat the bad guys—as if it's inevitable that only good guys win.

"For He will command His angels concerning you to guard you in all your ways; they will lift you up in their hands, so that you will not strike your foot against a stone."
~ Psalm 91:11-12

Chapter 18

When I wake up on Tuesday morning, I know what I have to do. So I pretend I'm doing strength-training and say that's why I'm riding my bike to school. I spend the day making lists in the margins of my notebooks of all the things I'll say to the police. I imagine the whole encounter in my head like it's a scene in a play.

We're starting to learn about debate in public speaking, and in chorus, kids are auditioning for solos in the upcoming winter concert. In art class, I spend time unleashing joy with shading and carefully calculated lines. We're studying Newton's Law in conceptual physics, sitting around the room in small groups with friction boards, trying to figure out which surfaces have the most and least drag.

Finally, at the end of the day, my English teacher wants us to try writing dystopian short stories. I fool around with a story about a girl who seems to be Native American living in maybe 800 or so AD, but as the story unfolds, the reader finds out it's really in the future. There's been some terrible nuclear war, and so we're back to Native Americans and open fields. The big shocking scene when the reader realizes it's the future is when the girl digs in the ground and finds a Darth Maul book bag from the twenty-first century. I work on this for an hour or so. Then I delete the whole thing.

Somehow, I go through the motions of high school life while simultaneously planning my visit to the Butler Police Department.

The show is this weekend, so we run the whole thing at rehearsal every day now, and I'm developing a better sense of the flow. My feelings about Lisa have changed a lot since September. I can remember being so scared of her and feeling intimidated by her beauty and her talent. Even if, girl to girl, we're still not friends, and even if my sisters still can't stand her, when I'm on stage with her, I totally trust her. Or I totally trust her when she's Annie. And I'm starting to think she feels the same way about me. After the run-through, when Ms. D's giving notes, Ms. D says as much, and we both steal glances at the other.

"That's what's at the heart of this show, girls," she says to the two of us, with everybody else watching. "The audience has to believe that Annie, miraculously, can swim down into the murky depths where Helen resides and bring her to the surface—to the world." I'm nodding, blushing. "Lisa, you make me feel like you're willing to drown for Helen. And Grace," she says, and turns all her attention to me, "you make me feel, in that moment when you're at the pump, like you're looking up to the surface and seeing sunshine for the very first time in your life." Ms. D kind of shakes her head and looks like she might cry. "Grace, you make me believe. Today, I didn't see a high school freshman named Grace. I saw Helen."

Even if I'm blushing so much my ears will just fall right off, I wouldn't trade this feeling of accomplishment for anything. I think about the essay I read by Helen Keller in September, and how Helen said the first thing she'd want to study if she had three days to see would be Annie Sullivan's face so she could look for physical evidence of those qualities Helen already knew about Annie so well. I remember, when I read it, in my imagination, I saw Lisa.

After rehearsal, I don't go looking for my sisters. I go outside to the bike rack, grab my bicycle, and head into town. It's cold, and the police station is further down the main drag than I imagined. But I eventually arrive. Once inside, an officer behind a glass window beckons me over.

"I . . . wanted to talk to someone about the boy who disappeared in Reisterstown on Sunday," I say.

I look around the front lobby. There's a woman with a little girl. They're reading *Hop on Pop* and don't seem to be paying any attention to me. The officer gets up and pushes a buzzer, and indicates I should come inside. He seems friendly and looks a little familiar. Our neighborhood has been crawling with police since Noah disappeared. He asks my name and introduces himself, and I do a lot of polite nodding.

Then he takes me to a room with a coffee machine and a table with some chairs, and gestures like I should sit. So I do. Another police officer, who looks familiar, too, enters, and so I jump up, and we go through introductions again. Fluorescent lights make the policemen look tired and a little green, and the room smells like burnt coffee.

"What can we do for you, Grace?" the first officer says.

"I think my neighbor could be involved in the disappearance of the boy from Reisterstown . . . um . . . who disappeared on Sunday." I'm not sure if I'm supposed to keep talking, or wait for them to ask me questions, so I wait.

They're both nodding at me, looking like they expect I'll continue, so I take a breath and do.

"I saw him . . . um . . . my neighbor, on Sunday night. It was really late, and he lives alone, and I think he had someone in his house with him. I saw people . . . I mean, him and somebody else, and then I heard about the boy in Reisterstown, and I'm worried . . . that if I don't say anything, you know, about what I saw . . ."

They're still not talking. I wish I knew which words would make everybody stop nodding and talking and go arrest Mr. Bowen.

"What is this neighbor's name?" asks Policeman One.

"Jason Bowen. He lives by himself. He came home in the middle of the night on Sunday, and I saw . . . or I think I saw someone else in his house, with him I mean." I think about my words. They're not painting the right picture. "I couldn't sleep, and I saw him come home. It was really late. Like two a.m. maybe." I think about what happened. "It was snowing," I add, not sure why I say this last part.

"Okay. So . . . you're worried that Jason Bowen might have the boy who disappeared in Reisterstown," Policeman One says.

I nod.

"Because you saw two people in his house, and you know he lives alone."

I nod again. Nobody says anything. Then I add, "He has a shed, and it's locked. He could have something in it. You know, like the guy in California. You know, the guy who had . . ."

"Right," One says again.

Or something like Noah's book bag, I think in my head.

"Where do you live, Grace?" asks the same guy. I wonder if the second guy is just a chaperone, or in training or something. I give my address, and he asks me a few more questions, like how long have I known my neighbor, and how old am I, and do my parents know where I am right now.

Then they're both standing and thanking me for being an interested citizen. I stand, too, and ask if they're going to look in the shed.

"We can't say right now, Grace, but we appreciate what you told us."

I feel like my trip was useless. I feel like they're ushering me out the door and thinking I'm a dumb, paranoid kid.

"I guess you need probable cause, right, to look in his shed. You need evidence?" By now we're all three of us standing, and I'm zipping up my jacket.

They tell me I'm right about that, but that it's always better to make reports, even if we lack concrete evidence, than stew over whether we should've said something or not.

Before I leave, the first guy says, "Is there anything else you want to talk about, Grace?"

"Noah Dunne is my neighbor," I blurt out. "He lives across the street from me, next door to Mr. Bowen. Right next door. Noah's the boy who disappeared in September."

"We know who Noah is, Grace."

I nod. "Right." I swallow. "Well, when Noah first disappeared, I saw the police all over the place, looking for him. And now I don't see you guys anymore. I'm thinking you gave up. And so the kidnapper got away with it. And now he's doing it again."

I figure now they'll tell me about what a terrific Cub Scout leader and Christian this guy is. And so generous with Christmas presents. And how I'm just a dumb kid who doesn't have a clue.

The second cop, the one who hasn't said anything, says something funny. "Trust us, okay? Sometimes things are not what they seem."

"He had a book bag in his living room on Halloween. Exactly like Noah's."

They nod.

"What happened to it?" Number One says.

"No idea," I say. "Maybe he wrapped it up and gave it to the church."

I ride home as fast as I can, replaying in my head what happened at the police station. I barely stuttered. I cut through the high school and over the footbridge so it's a shorter ride home. I'm riding as fast as I can, and I stand up to keep from totally running out of steam as I ride my bike to the top of the footbridge. But I'm really worn out, so I finally get off and walk it for a bit. As I'm walking with my bike, I scan the stream and woods below. This would be a good place to throw Noah's book bag, right? Bowen wouldn't even have to go down into the woods. He could throw it from up here. I remember the kid with the trash bag. Did that happen before or after Halloween? After, right? No, wait. I'm not sure. But who was that kid? I should go back and tell the police about that too. I get back on my bike and go home as fast as I can. But Mom is still upset.

"How could it take so long to ride home from school?" she wants to know. I tell her rehearsal ran long, and that I must be out of shape.

"Why do you even have a phone, Gracie? You *never* turn it on."

After dinner, Dad watches the news, my brothers take showers, and the rest of us help wash dishes and put plates away.

"Hey, Mae! Look at this!" Dad yells from the family room. "Quick!"

Mom puts a dish on the counter and goes to see what Dad is so excited to show her. Nana, my sisters, and I follow. The headline flashing across the screen reads, "Missing Reisterstown boy found," and there's footage of a boy with his parents sitting on a couch that looks a lot like ours. The boy and his mother are hugging, and the dad is kind of patting his son on the back. The boy's hair is pretty much completely hiding his face, and the dad is telling a reporter what sounds like a convoluted story about how his son was at

some nameless relative's house, and how it was all a big mistake.

"Drugs!" Dad declares, punching my mother's arm and pushing her off the arm of the sofa.

"John! Take it easy."

My dad blames drugs whenever someone's behavior seems sketchy. And now he grabs Mom and sits her on his lap. "See, Mae? No bodysnatchers here, okay?" And he looks at me. "See, baby?"

Before I fall asleep, I try to make sense of my . . . disappointment. Am I really *sorry* Mr. Bowen didn't kidnap some other innocent kid? No, I decide, really sleepy at this point. I just want people to believe me that he took Noah. I look over at my sisters. Mary's snoring, and Bridget's buried under her covers, a blue light glowing through the blanket—she's texting. I grab my sketch pad from under my bed and turn to a new page. The deadline for the art show is Friday, and I'm moving along on my picture of the children with the angels. But there's another image searing itself onto my brain. I plug in my Christmas lights, flip to a fresh page, and start drawing. This time, the images in my head flow on to the page easily.

On the way home from school on Wednesday, I ask Becca if we can stop by the footbridge because I think I lost money riding my bike home. It's a dumb lie, but since nobody is really listening too intently, I get away with it. I jump out of the car and sprint down to the water's edge, to the spot I remember seeing the kid. I look across the stream to the spot where I saw the Christmas paper. Nothing. I walk up and down along the water's edge, kicking leaves out of the way. I guess I was wrong.

I'm utterly shocked when I get out of Becca's car at home. Across the backyards, two police officers are standing with Mr. Bowen while he opens his shed. My surprise makes me forget stealth, and I stand there and gawk while Mary and Bridget walk into the house. I just can't believe it. First of all, I didn't think those two guys were taking me seriously. But more importantly, I thought the boy who'd disappeared turned up. So why are they searching Mr. Bowen's shed? What does this mean? I'm so excited, imagining clues they'll find inside. I'm betting the book bag I saw in the house is in the shed, and maybe a lunch box or a jacket. But mainly, this means they're on to him. I feel enormous waves of relief. I'm not alone.

By now Becca's car has pulled out of our driveway, and I'm just standing halfway down our hill on the steps. Mr. Bowen has unlocked the padlock, and the three of them step inside. If he keeps his shed anything like how he keeps his house, it's neat as a pin, and clues will present themselves easily. Moments pass. I realize I'm exposed, so I run down the rest of the steps, sit on the bottom one, and pull up my hood. Then I scoot closer to a bush to camouflage myself more.

The three emerge from the shed, the police officers first and Mr. Bowen last. He turns and locks the padlock. It doesn't look like they're arresting him. I stay where I am, cold, but too curious to go inside.

"Gracie? Gracie!" Mom calls down the hill, way too loud. "Gracie?"

Mr. Bowen looks toward our house.

I stand up. "Coming," I call back as softly as I can.

Once in the house, I immediately volunteer to walk Sweetie. I put her leash on her and almost run back outside and down the hill. I can't tell if the police car is still in his driveway, so I walk further down the street. As Sweetie and I cross the street, the police car pulls out of Mr. Bowen's driveway. As far as I can tell, he's not in the backseat. I turn around to walk home. And hear footsteps. Getting closer.

Sweetie barks, and I stop.

"Walking the dog, huh?" Bowen crosses the road. He's dressed like he's jogging, but as he reaches the sidewalk and places himself between me and the remaining distance to my back door, he plants his feet and doesn't appear to be going on much of an evening run.

I nod. Sweetie barks again.

"Hey, girl," he says gently and kneels down to pet her. She sniffs him, and I'm reminded of the day the first week of school when she ran away. I remember thinking it was odd that she sniffed him like he had a dog. He doesn't. Does he? If he doesn't, what is she smelling?

I pull her away and try to walk around him. But he stands up quickly.

"Grace, do you have something you want to talk to me about?"

"No."

He nods his head, appraising me, looking like he's trying not to laugh.

"Okay. I just . . . I think you sure do like talking *about* me to other people, don't you?" he asks. Not in a mean way, more like he thinks this whole situation is terrifically funny.

"I have to go," I say, panic starting to disable me. "My parents know I'm walking the dog, and they'll be out here looking for me. M-m-m-my . . . m-m-m—"

"Don't get your panties in a bunch, little girl," Mr. Bowen says and lights a cigarette.

I get past him while he's lighting a match. I'm ten feet past him when he calls after me. "If ever you *do* want to talk, you know where I live." He smiles, like he's inviting me to tea.

I back away, knowing I'm almost home, but I feel like I have to keep my eye on him so he doesn't run up behind me and burn me with his cigarette or something.

As I start up our steps, he says, "I know where you live too."

***

Clementine watches Bowen walk back inside the house that isn't a home, and follows him. She watches as he finds the gun he hides under Christmas presents, places onto it a device that will silence the noise of the blast, and runs back up the stairs while hiding the gun by the small of his back. When he opens the back door and steps outside, she still follows, and when his disgusting, slimy bodyguards shove her to the ground, Clementine shoves back as hard as she can. The demons stop laughing. They register surprise, actually, even if it's just for a second. But it's long enough for something to happen to her. She's bigger and more solid.

"Grace will not die tonight," she says to them and rushes to Bowen, who by now is striding across his backyard. He stops and knits his brow, looks to the road, and then to Grace's window. Is he figuring out how to kill her? He stands still, and then walks to the shed, digging into a pocket for a key, and unlocks it. He crouches down in a far corner and pulls up a loosened floorboard. Clementine stands at the door, not wanting to be alone in a small space with him—or his demons. He pulls out some newspaper clippings and a dirt-covered child's sweater, and sits on the floor. The clippings are old and yellowed. He reads. After a while, Clementine moves inside and looks over his shoulder. The boy's face in the photo, worn and faded now, smiles at a camera, oblivious to the purpose that pose would serve.

Bowen gets up, holding his trophies, and takes matches out of a pocket. He locks the shed and walks toward the running path behind his house, into the woods. A police car drives down the street, slowly.

"Grace will not die tonight," Clementine whispers to the man.

Clutching the treasures, he seems to be conflicted as to whether or not he wants to burn them. Still holding them, he goes back inside the house.

The angel waits.

.

"I wonder what becomes of lost opportunities? Perhaps our guardian angel gathers them up as we drop them, and will give them back to us in the beautiful sometime when we have grown wiser, and learned how to use them rightly."
~ Helen Keller

Chapter 19

I go through the 'scholarly' motions on Wednesday, speaking, or singing, or painting, as needed, but really, all I'm thinking about is getting into the auditorium at 3:00 and rehearsing *The Miracle Worker* for the second to last time. When I finally do, I'm even more excited. Kids are walking around in costume, and others are wearing headsets and are busy maneuvering cordless microphones onto people's bodies. The light crew is here, and they're on ladders focusing lights and adjusting colored gels that make the stage look like nighttime and early morning, and it all looks just plain cool. Our whole set is done and just about painted. A couple of boys are moving the platform that includes Annie's bedroom and the stairs that lead up to it. They pull out tape that glows in the dark and mark a place on the stage where the platform will sit.

It's an absolutely hectic zoo, and I love it.

Marty sees me. He has a headset on, and he's carrying his script in a big binder.

"Grace! Costume!" he says, and points backstage. I nod and run backstage, then out the door, finding a rack full of clothes in the hall and a couple of moms talking to cast members about hems and quick costume changes. I think about how much fun all this would be for Mom. Why didn't I volunteer her to help with costumes? Next time I will. The moms try my jumper on me, and it fits perfectly. I take it, and get dressed.

There's lots of business with microphone checks and talk about microphone dos and don'ts. I'm glad I don't use one. Cast members are passing around medical tape to secure the mics to their faces.

Marty calls, "Places!" He now has a crew of seven or eight kids, and he's ordering everyone around. I really tried to get Pearl and Morgan to be on stage crew. Pearl said she couldn't get a ride. Morgan just said no. But these kids all look like they're having a lot of fun, and I promise myself to try harder to involve my friends next time.

It's a great first full dress run. It's the first time Lisa has actually had a second story window to climb out of, and we're all excited backstage when she's climbing down the ladder and talking to Mr. Keller, aka Zach. And it's the first time we have running water coming out of the pump. One of the kids said Ms. D's husband worked on the pump all weekend.

I'm thrilled. I feel like, all of a sudden, it's real—like we're actually going to *do* this. People are really going to come and see it.

When I go backstage to wait on what I now like to call "Helen's chair", I watch Marty flirting with one of the girls on stage crew—I mean, *really* flirting. It aggravates me to think about how Lisa is literally twenty feet away at this very minute. She could just glance backstage and see him and be really upset.

Since we're running the whole show with lights and sound and costumes, we run later than 5 p.m. Mary and Bridget finish their practice before I do mine, so they come and sit in the back for the last half hour or so of the show. I peek out and see them, and I see Caleb sitting there too. I haven't talked to him since Noah's 5K, so I feel really glad he'd want to watch, even for just a little bit. Afterward, I walk to the back of the auditorium to find my sisters. Caleb is gone.

Thursday's pretty much the same, except maybe worse. I present myself to all my teachers, and I try to participate and do my work, but as I get closer to opening night, I'm so incredibly excited about the show that class becomes a terrible study in endurance. Sleeping is crazy too. I've been madly tossing and turning every night. One night, I dream it's opening night, and as the curtain opens, I realize I never went to any rehearsals, and I just stand in shock. Another night, I dream there's no set. Crazy stuff. Marty keeps annoying me with his backstage antics. I notice him touching Caroline's hair in a really familiar, kind of boyfriendish way as he's talking to her. Then I see him up in the lighting booth looking pretty amorous with a girl on the lighting crew.

"Why is he doing this to Lisa?" I ask Leo at one point on Thursday night.

Leo shrugs. "It's his mission to make out with every female at Butler. I think he's pretty much past the halfway mark."

I laugh.

"I'm not kidding. It's a bet."

Driving home with Dad on Thursday night, it hits me that when I wake up on Friday morning, it'll be opening night. I feel so pumped up I'm afraid I'll oversleep and be late for school. And if anyone is late, Ms. D has told us multiple times, we'll be ineligible to perform. It will have all been for nothing. I have to get up, which means I have to go to sleep. I close my eyes, and as I'm wrapping my blanket around me, I decide that to make myself sleepy, I'll imagine the show. I'll play it like a movie in my head.

I start with scene one and imagine the whole opening part when the Kellers find out about Helen. I'm watching it as if I'm sitting on top of a ladder right on the stage. I can see baby Helen in her crib, suddenly not seeing or hearing, and I think about how scared Helen must have been—I mean, when she was born she *had* all her senses. And then she got sick, and all of a sudden everything got so quiet and dark.

At some point in my movie, I lose the thread of the real play, and I'm not watching it from the ladder anymore. I *am* Helen now, and I start doing things that are different from the script. I'm running away from home, I mean from the Kellers' house, and even though I know Helen is supposed to be blind, as I run I start to *see* all kinds of things—things that are kind of out of focus, but bright, almost neon. It looks like I've arrived at a carnival, or maybe some kind of traveling circus. The edges of things are skewed, distorted, like wearing glasses with the wrong prescription. And I can hear, too, even though I'm supposed to be deaf. Everything sounds like I'm hearing underwater, but I catch parts of words, especially vowels. I hear a lot of vowels. I try to recognize people. I'm young, and everybody else seems really old.

137

At one point, I arrive at a merry-go-round, and it's a little creepy. It's moving, and there's music, but I'm hearing the music like it's distorted, too, and the horses are all these weird neon colors, and the edges of the horses keep growing and then shrinking. But I step onto it and walk around it, and I see people. At first, they're mainly characters in the play, and people who are working on it. Then I start seeing other people, like Bridget is there, and Mom, and Hayden is there too. I think I see Mr. Bowen with Noah on one horse, but when I look again, it's Marty with Lisa.

I get off the merry-go-round, or really fall off, and I feel someone's hand trying to help me up. I turn to see who it is, and my eyesight seems to get more normal after whoever it is touched me, and I can hear normally too. It's like the person's touch healed me. I stand up, and I don't think I'm a little girl anymore. I think I'm myself now. And I am looking at Helen Keller. But she's a grown-up. She's definitely older than me. She smiles at me, and tears well up in her eyes. She takes her right hand and places it up to her lips and places the back of it into the palm of her left hand.

I know that sign means "Thank you", so I say, "You're welcome!" Then she takes both my hands and places them on her throat so I can feel the vibrations.

"Water," she says. But she doesn't sound like someone who's been deaf all her life. She sounds like me.

"You can talk!" I say.

She laughs a happy, natural-sounding laugh. "You're my voice, Grace."

I wake up, flat on my back, my cheeks all wet. I look at the clocks. 5:30 a.m.

"Thank you," I whisper to God, and maybe to the spirit of Helen Keller too. I'll not oversleep today. I sit up in bed and greet the big day.

I'm sitting in chorus, thinking about last night's final dress and Helen's face in my dream. I've seen lots of pictures of her, all of them black and white. She's a little girl in most of them, but I've seen pictures of her as an older lady too. But my dream was in color, and Helen was maybe twenty-five. She looked pretty, and I just don't think I have any pictures like the way Helen looked in my dream. I guess I made this up on my own. It seemed so real.

We're singing the "Halleluiah Chorus" for the concert next month. Morgan elbows me. I forgot to sing with the altos. I look at the clock. It's 10:00. Ten hours 'til show time. I let myself float away to Helen's quiet place. I'm outside by the water pump. I imagine the feeling in my fingers of the vibrations Annie is making in her throat. "Wa-ter." I reach for the pump and connect the vibrations I feel to the water. It's like I'm some sole survivor of a race of people who live underground—and I just found a narrow path to the rest of the world. I have a word. I want to scream it. And I would, except Marty is calling my name. I look up, feeling embarrassed. What's he doing here? My chorus teacher is nodding and shooing me with her free hand while she plunks out notes with the other. Marty is carrying a pass, and after he hands it to me, I follow him into the hall.

Once outside, he's laughing and puts his arm around me, walking me away from my class. I think about Lisa and what she'd do to me if she saw her boyfriend's arm around yet another girl. I step away.

"So what's up?" I say. I'm learning "S" is a good starting-a-sentence sound for me.

"I want to show you something, Gracie."

Since when is Marty calling me Gracie? This is all pretty weird. But I follow him down the hall and past the main office. I see Julie walking into the principal's office with her dad and a police officer, the same guy who used to be in our neighborhood so much right after Noah disappeared. I stop.

"Come on," Marty says.

I look at Marty, then back through the glass at the Dunnes. That sensation I get when I look at something and it feels like some curtain is being lifted washes over me. I see in Mr. Dunne's face that he thinks Noah is dead. I see images, an afterglow of something. I close my eyes. I see a sweatshirt. It's covered in leaves.

Marty takes my hand and walks faster. As we reach the prop room, he pulls a key out from his jean pocket, and we're in. He closes the door but doesn't turn on the light.

"I just wanted to tell you that you nailed it last night," he says, leaning against the door in the darkened room.

"Why are we in here?"

"You're beautiful, Grace." Marty reaches for my shoulder and gently pulls me to him.

I think about all the girls I've been watching Marty flirt with this week when he's supposed to be someone's boyfriend. And then I notice the worst thing. He's blocking my only way out.

"What? Am I next on your list?" I say, and I can hear the panic in my voice.

He laughs at me and wraps his arms tighter around me. "What list?"

He takes my face in his hands and starts kissing me—not the way Caleb kissed me, and not the way I imagined Marty would kiss a girl all these months I thought he was such a prize. And then that other me—the one who clobbered Connor Myers in seventh grade—shows up. First, I step on his foot, hard, and then I punch him, but not in the nose this time. I think I catch him somewhere along his jawline. I grab the doorknob before he grabs my arm. We play this kind of silent tug-of-war in the doorway.

"Tease," he says in this low, gravelly voice that really scares me. Then I'm out. I run down the hall. I just want to be near people. Once I'm out of the drama wing and back in the main hall, I stop running. What do I do now? Go to the principal? Go home? I can't leave school. If I sign out early, I won't be allowed to perform tonight. I think about the bet. I wonder what number I was on his list. What a loser. Him, that is. Not me.

My feet take me back to the main office. I pretend I have a reason to be here, and then I remember the pass Marty gave me. I pull it out of my pocket. It's a Guidance pass. I wonder how he snagged a guidance pass. It occurs to me he's a peer facilitator this period. Ironic. I walk down the hall, heading toward Guidance—kind of improvising in my mind about what I'll do when I get there, and I walk past the principal's office. I see Julie and her dad. I look in, and Julie's dad is helping her to stand up. Julie sees me and unravels.

She steps into the hall, and I wrap my arms around her. Her dad is still saying something to the principal. I feel her body convulsing with sobs, and I start crying too. No one has told me Noah died, but I feel chills all over my body. The ripping noise is all I can hear.

Snapshots. That's what I'm getting from Julie. Still images stored in her mind. Things Julie saw. Pages from Noah's take-home folder. Notebooks with his name on them—in a pile, dirty, dried mud covering them, ripped pages. Someone gave the contents of his book bag to his parents. They'd been recovered from the woods, buried beneath the leaves. And a sweatshirt. Noah's red sweatshirt. And an action figure. Anakin Skywalker. With a great big slash mark across it. The Dunnes probably think someone hurt him in our woods. My guess is, sometime between Halloween and now, Mr. Bowen tossed Noah's stuff into the woods and just waited for it to be found. So where's the book bag? And where's Noah?

Then I get that paranoid feeling like someone's watching me, and I'm afraid to open my eyes.

But I do. And there stands Noah—or that same transparent shadow of him I saw the day after he disappeared—looking at me, but no, not really. He's looking at Julie and their dad. As I step away, Julie and Mr. Dunne make their way down the hall, and I steal another look at Noah. He looks worried—not sad really, just concerned. I remember the way he looked when the bus took us back to school after he smashed all the kids' heads with his lunch box, and the principal said he was on bus probation. Noah probably didn't even know what the word meant. He just knew his parents would be mad. And he had that same look—like somebody he loved was going to get hurt, and he couldn't stop it. Then he looks straight at me, intensely, like he's trying to say something, but he doesn't have words. Even if he did talk, I wouldn't hear him. The ripping noise is deafening. So I just stand there. And then he's gone.

The principal wants to know if I need something. I want to ask him why the Dunnes are in his office, if they found Noah's notebooks and sweatshirt in the woods by our house, and if they arrested Jason Bowen. He asks again. I shake my head, back away, and walk back to chorus class.

It's evening, almost show time. I wish I was Helen. I could live in my own world and make it look however I want it to. I wouldn't hear people cry or the sky rip apart. And I wouldn't see things that don't make any sense.

I hear the 5:00 news in the family room. I'm having tomato soup by myself in the kitchen, and then Dad will drive me over to school. I'm listening for news about Noah. If he died, wouldn't it be on TV? I mean, if someone found evidence, wouldn't there be a story? Why else was Mr. Dunne taking Julie out of school? But I hear nothing. No story about any items found in the woods. Nothing. It's like the police forgot him.

I'm so confused. What did I see? Did I see Noah? My head is pounding. I'm trying not to cry, as our house is Grand Central Station tonight. They'll all think I'm nervous about the play when, actually, I'm not. I'm too busy trying to figure out what Noah, or whoever I saw, wants. Is he dead? Is he locked up somewhere? Boy, I'd so rather be wrestling Marty in the prop room than trying to interpret what some bizarre kind of shadow of a missing boy is asking me to do.

Dad drives me to school.

"Any news about Noah, Dad?"

"What do you mean? Today?"

"Mr. Dunne was with Julie at school. I think they got bad news."

"How so?"

"Julie was crying, and I just . . ."

"No, baby." Dad shakes his head. "I didn't hear anything. But it's almost three months, Gracie. I'm guessing they're not going to find him. It's just been too long." He looks over at me. We drive in silence for a while. I look out the passenger window so Dad can't see the tears rolling down my cheeks. Part of me is thinking the same thing Dad's thinking. It's just been too long.

"Are you ready for tonight?" he says. "Any . . ." He seems momentarily stumped. "Any opening night jitters?"

"No," I say, still looking away. I love my dad. Sometimes when he talks to me, I imagine he's this explorer, trailblazing through some undiscovered country, and he's madly chopping away at all these vines that make it so hard to find a path—and there's a really well-marked one just around the corner, but he's hacking away at this one, just because it's the only path that leads to me. I know he's totally out of his element with this drama thing. Give John O'Shaunessy seed times or stopwatches, and he's in his element, but this play stuff has him tongue-tied. But he's trying. And I love him for that.

"Do you think the police are still looking?"

"Yeah. Yeah, I do. I think after the first couple of weeks it becomes a different kind of investigation, but yeah, I do."

I look out the window and up at the night stars. Maybe I'm just imagining, but I feel like I'm seeing not hundreds but more like thousands of miniscule wings, as far as I can see. I blink. Still there.

When I get to school, I pretend I don't feel incredibly awkward talking to Marty. He behaves likewise. Of course, he probably *doesn't* feel awkward. I'm guessing that forcing himself on girls is a hobby with him, or a sport.

And then it's show time. We join hands for an opening night prayer. It's probably illegal in a public school, but kudos to Ms. D for doing it anyway. We pray to Saint Genesius, who, she explains, is the patron saint of actors. We do a power squeeze around the circle of cast and crew, and then Marty calls, "Places!" and it starts.

Scene follows scene. First, I hate Annie. I resent what's happening to Helen. Slowly, I wake up to a world that lets me speak. By the end, when I say "water", I'm sobbing. All the work I did trying to find my epiphany so I could connect to Helen's moment of remembering words feels like castles in the sand now. In this moment, I'm just Helen with Annie. And I'm crying because I can speak. My face is soaked.

I imagine myself carrying Helen with me from scene to scene, inviting her to touch my face to read my expressions, so she could know this play that was written about her life. In her essay, she talked about the actor, Joseph Jefferson, who was famous for playing Rip Van Winkle when she was alive. One night, he took her through his performance, allowing her to read it with her fingers. I mean, scene by scene, she was right there on stage with him, feeling his cheeks and his lips. He let her fingers serve as eyes. I'd love to do that for her. I'd love to give her *The Miracle Worker* that way.

During the curtain call, I'm still crying a little bit. I think this worries Lisa, so I make myself stop. I'm so happy. It's so funny that after a day of the clock ticking so slowly, tonight's two hours of performance is just a blur.

When it's over, I go back to the girls' dressing room, feeling a jumbled-up mixture of bliss and exhaustion, and kind of shy about working my way through the crowd to find my family. I'm back in my jeans and sweatshirt when the door opens. Bridget peeks in.

"Gracie, hurry up. Papa Da's here. And so is everybody else." She walks in and hugs me. "You were excellent." And then again, "Hurry up."

The door closes behind her. I grab my stuff to follow. When I step out into the hall, I'm surprised by how packed it is. It's an ocean of families, all hugging their kids, and bouquets of flowers are being passed around. Way down the hall, I see Mr. Bowen. That stops me short. I register that I'm on the first floor. I could easily leap out the window if he's here to kill me. Why is he here, at a high school play? He has no good reason to be here.

But it doesn't matter. This is my golden opportunity. If he's here, he's *not* home. Stuffing any logical naysaying into the back pocket of my mind, I step backward and run into the girls' dressing room, open the window, and jump out onto the grass. On my tiptoes, I close the window again, so when Bridget bursts back in two minutes from now, totally impatient, she won't immediately figure me out. And then I run. In socks. This is probably not my best idea.

It's only three miles to our house if I take the footbridge. So it's like a 5K. If I make good time, I should get to Mr. Bowen's house before him. I stop and rip off my socks and stick them in my sweatshirt pocket. The ground is cold, but now I can run faster. It's so dark. There are no stars anymore, or wings—just cloud cover. I keep running. I have to get inside Mr. Bowen's house before he gets home. I have to know if he took Noah. If there's a single thing of Noah's in his house, I'll find it this time.

"Although the world is full of suffering, it is also full of the overcoming of it."
~ Helen Keller

Chapter 20

My phone is vibrating in my pocket. I pull it out—it's Dad. Oh, boy. Do I answer? Do I tell him I'm out and about, playing Agent 007? I press the button on the side to ignore the call instead. I climb under Mr. Bowen's fence and run across the yard to his back door. Everything is dark. I turn the knob. Of course, it's locked. I feel scared about walking around to the front door. What would I say if someone saw me trying to get into his house at 11:00 at night? I run around to the front and walk up on his porch. Nailed to his front door is a cartoon turkey smiling at me. The front door is locked too. What was I thinking? I remember the basement window. Before I can stop myself, I'm skirting past bushes and climbing into the basement. The window well smells like wet leaves and worms, and some kind of rose bush scratches my cheek as I squeeze inside. I glance over to the Dunnes' house. I don't see Julie watching me. Then I jump down, and I'm in.

It's really dark in here, and I almost scream when a grandfather clock somewhere starts chiming. It's coming from upstairs, probably the dining room. I tiptoe forward, using my phone as a flashlight. No Christmas presents anymore, anywhere. I wonder where he put them. Christmas is still a month away. Did he take them to the church like the priest said he would? Would that have happened already? I don't see anything that looks too out of place—boxes, an ironing board, boogie boards. Wait a minute, boogie boards are totally out of place. It's hard to imagine Mr. Bowen on a boogie board, but this isn't the kind of hard evidence I need. I need something of Noah's. It smells musty down here, but not like anything bad has happened. I get down on my hands and knees with my phone held out in front of me, madly looking for a clue. Clear as a bell, I hear the white-haired lady's voice. I recognize it from the day Noah disappeared, and, I realize, from his backyard last week.

Noah wasn't down here.

I stop. Oh. Mr. Bowen never brought Noah *down here*. Upstairs. He never brought Noah down here, but Noah was upstairs. So I go.

Every hair on my body stands on end. Every bit of me is charged with electricity — but I go upstairs anyway. I realize as I climb the stairs that I'm leaving my escape hatch behind. I reach the first floor. It's pitch black. I pretend I'm Helen as I feel my way across the hall into a bedroom, afraid to use my phone because I know I'm going to get caught now. I feel a dresser, and some coins on top. As my night vision adjusts, I see this is probably Mr. Bowen's room. Maybe there's a clue in here, but a magnet is pulling me to the spare bedroom, so I leave this one behind. I think about the way the Dunnes' house is laid out. It's the same model. All the bedrooms are along this hall. I feel my way into the bathroom. Wrong room. Then I step inside the last room. It's small and neat. In the Dunnes' house, this is Noah's room. I quietly close the door and pan the room with my phone. I see nothing.

Headlights light up the far corner of the room. A car is pulling into Mr. Bowen's driveway. I freeze—literally. Whatever survival sense I thought I'd display in this situation is failing me. As I hear the front door open, I dive under the bed and hit my head. I don't breathe or move or even open my eyes. And time passes. I know time passes because my legs and the back of my neck start to really hurt. I take in air with my nose, and open one eye just a smidgen. It's inky black under here. I open the other eye and hope my sight will adjust like it did in the basement. Every once in a while I hear footsteps. And plates. Is he in the kitchen? I'm trying to figure out whether I could jump out this window without him seeing me if he's putting dishes away in the kitchen. For some reason, I can't get my brain to focus on where the kitchen is in relation to this room. I wait until I hear him moving again, and then I hear a TV. So he's in his living room, I guess. Does he have a TV in his bedroom? I wish I'd noticed that. I wait a long time, a *really* long time. I listen to beginnings and ends of shows. Even though it's still on, I'm thinking by now he might've fallen asleep and left the TV on. My legs are cramping up under here. I think about all the books and movies I've consumed in my life where kids wind up in this situation. You have to escape or you die. I ever so slowly try sliding out from under the bed, and my eye picks up something shimmering on the floor near the dresser. I slide on my tummy to get a closer look. It's another one of those long white feathers. And next to it is Anakin's little plastic hand—with a madcap crazy long scratch. I suck in breath—making noise and slamming my head again. I grab the hand. Isn't this evidence? Hard evidence? Proof he had Noah here? I climb out from under the bed, open the window as quietly as I can, and jump.

I run out onto the street, fast. I feel prickly tentacles grabbing at me, and even though I know they're not real, that feeling just makes me run faster.

I run in the back door, clutching Anakin's hand. My parents are standing in the kitchen. Nana and Papa Da are sitting at the table. Everyone looks up at once.

"Where the hell were you?" Dad screams.

"Grace!" Mom says at the same time. Nana and Papa Da stand up.

"Saints preserve us!" Papa Da says.

I hear elephants running down the stairs, or maybe it's my siblings. And then in walks Officer What's His Name, followed by my brothers and sisters, all poking their heads around him and contorting their necks to get a look at what happened. I have a new appreciation for the word rubbernecking.

He looks at me and takes a deep breath.

"Tragedy averted," he says to the group at large.

"It's almost one o'clock in the morning!" Mom says, looking about as upset as I've ever seen her.

Before I can stop myself, before I can self-censor, I open my hand. Sobbing without making any sound, releasing the terror I held inside for the last hour or so under Mr. Bowen's bed, I try to form words. Everybody stops screaming, or really moving at all. Sean steps forward first.

"Where'd you get that?" he says. The police guy is right behind him. He looks at Anakin's hand, and then at me. "Where'd you find it, Gracie?" he asks again.

"M-m-m . . ."

"What the h...," says Mary.

"Mary!" Mom says, momentarily sparing me everyone's collective gaze.

I force my lips apart, and blurt out, "Mr. Bowen's house." They all look dumbfounded.

"What?" Dad says. "What are you talking about?" Everyone looks confused, except Sean and the police guy. They get what this means. I can tell they do. Their faces make the dam inside me break, and I start crying out loud. Not good. Once I really let go and start wailing, it's hard for me to stop.

Everything is happening at once. The police guy—Officer Bingham, my mother is calling him—holds my arms and leans down to look at me. He is really tall. My parents and grandparents are all busy asking one another what the action figure hand means. My sisters are yelling at my parents to calm down. My brother Peter is saying something about hysteria over the rest of the din. Shea and Sean are staring at the hand.

Officer Bingham walks me out of the kitchen into the family room. He sits me down on the couch and positions himself next to me. He's talking softly now. I'm not crying so much now as hiccupping and kind of hyperventilating.

"Grace." He says my name in a way that they probably teach police use when talking people off window ledges. "What do you mean, 'Mr. Bowen's house'?"

I close my eyes and try to calm down. I try to take deep breaths like Ms. D taught us at rehearsal. I imagine my white-haired friend and pretend she's sitting here next to me. I imagine I'm really Helen, not Grace, and I'm totally protected from this place of sights and sounds. I imagine all is well. I open my eyes. It all comes out in a breath and a whisper.

"I went to his house. I was looking for evidence. I . . ."

He cuts me off. "Wait a minute. Did he know you were in his house?"

"He was at the play. I saw him."

"So you broke in?"

"Yeah."

"How?"

"Basement."

"Why?"

"Because . . . he . . . I found Anakin's hand under the bed. When I . . ."

"What bed? Slow down, girlfriend. I don't understand . . ."

"He took Noah, and I'm trying to find him, and I'm scared he killed . . ." and I'm crying again. I cover my face.

He leans in and speaks even more softly. "Why do you think he did this?"

Warm tears wash my cheeks and burn the cut I got on my cheek when I broke into the basement. They splash down onto my hair, my sweatshirt, Anakin's hand. "I just know," I whisper.

Officer Bingham is on the phone, turning the little action figure hand over in his big policeman hand. He keeps looking at me, like he's trying to figure something out, and then he goes back to the hand. I watch him trace the gash across the middle of Anakin's hand. Then he talks to my parents, and my brother Peter helps Papa Da upstairs. Everybody else is sitting around in the living room like they're waiting for the second act to start. Officer Bingham comes back to me in the family room and sits down next to me on the couch. My parents stand nearby—Mom reaches out and takes Dad's hand. In the moment before Officer Bingham speaks, I know something bad is going down.

"Grace, I have to arrest you for breaking and entering." I'm stunned. I guess my parents already knew because they don't seem surprised, just upset.

What follows next is a blur. Officer Bingham puts me in his police car, in the backseat like I'm a criminal. My parents follow behind in our car. When we get to the police station, Mom, Dad, and I wait in a small room while Officer Bingham does whatever red tape paperwork is involved in arresting somebody. Before this week, when I came here on my bike, I'd been to the police station once before in my whole life. Mom was Shea's Cub Scout leader, and we took a tour of the police barracks. But everything's different now. It all feels a lot different when you're on a tour versus being the criminal. Dad is talking to Mom about getting a lawyer. I'm not sure why I need one. I hadn't thought going into Mr. Bowen's basement was a crime—more a means to an end.

Mom leans over to me. "Before he comes back, Gracie, I want you to explain to Dad and me why you broke into Mr. Bowen's house." Her voice sounds stiff, kind of like she's reading cue cards.

"He leaves his window open, Mom. It wasn't locked. I didn't 'break' . . ."

"Okay, stop," Dad says. He wants us all to be quiet, but after a second he's talking himself. "What the hell were you thinking? Talk to me!"

I look at them. I had *tried* to talk—to my parents, the police, the priest, even Caleb. I've been trying for two and a half months, and I just didn't know what else to do. I didn't want to make more trouble. I just wanted to save Noah.

When I was little—post-playground incident, I guess—I made trouble for my parents constantly. Once, my mom picked me up from daycare, and they had me waiting with one of the teacher's aides in the lobby. I was still crying when Mom got there. Apparently, they had been watching *Flick*, a movie about a dog, and it was all too unbearably sad for little Grace. In elementary school, my parents got called in for conferences three or four different times because, as my teachers said, I was too sensitive for my own good. When I was in sixth grade, my Sunday School teacher thought there was something really unhinged about me when she was walking us through the Stations of the Cross during Lent. We got to the station where Jesus fell down under the weight of the cross, and she was trying to describe how heavy the cross was. I burst into tears. I remember her whispering to my mom about me.

"Is there something . . ." and then she paused like she didn't want to sound rude. Then she finished with, "*about* Grace that I should know about?" I was so embarrassed. Worse, I felt ashamed. I felt like I was weak, like being soft made me inferior.

Even the whole thing with Morgan when she moved in made my second-grade teacher tell my parents I might need some special help.

I tried to toughen up, to not let myself enter in so much. But it's like trying to breathe without air or fly without wings. I can't live in my body without entering in.

So now I'm in jail. My parents are waiting for me to explain. I know Dad's not actually mad so much as frustrated because he can't fix this. And he's probably peeved that I didn't forget about Mr. Bowen when he told me to.

"I know Mr. Bowen took Noah," I say.

"How?" they both say.

"I . . . see it."

Mom sighs and Dad groans.

"Grace. Make me understand. What do you mean you *see* things? Surely you can understand this is difficult to accept," says Officer Bingham. "You say *you saw* Noah being taken away by Jason Bowen the morning *after* he disappeared? But it was a . . . vision? Is that what you're telling me? You mean, what? You were hallucinating? Did you take something, some kind of drug, something you shouldn't have?"

I've been taken into a different room from Mom and Dad. I got fingerprinted and had my picture taken. I hope it won't be in tomorrow's paper. I was secretly imagining there'd be a picture of me as Helen Keller in tomorrow's paper. I'd rather grab my fifteen minutes of fame as Grace the actress than Grace the thief, or worse, Grace the crazy. We're in a room with a mirror. I'm sure it's one of those two-way mirrors they have on all the detective shows. In fact, I remember looking at it from the other side when we took our Cub Scout tour. There's another police officer in the room, too, but he's not saying anything. Another trainee, I guess.

I look into Officer Bingham's eyes. I'm tongue-tied. How can I explain what I see? Every time I've tried to tell someone, I hit a wall. Officer Bingham seems safe enough. I mean, I don't feel like he's a bad guy. I did get this creepy feeling when we were at the house, when he was on the phone, that he was thinking I could be the one who did something to Noah, that maybe that's why I showed up with the hand that matches the action figure's scratch. I watched that thought occur to him. But when I look at him now, I don't sense that he feels that way about me. I trust him, maybe not enough to say that I know the police have the rest of Anakin in an evidence bag somewhere with Noah's school books, and that it has a scratch that matches this one exactly—that I saw that in my mind too. I don't trust him enough to say that I know the police found the contents of Noah's book bag in the woods somewhere. No, I'm not going to shout out that stuff yet, but at least this guy makes me feel like he's listening.

Suddenly, I know why he's so familiar-looking. I look at his eyes and his face, and I realize. The right words fall on me like manna from Heaven, and I start talking, and this little thought kind of dances across my brain that I'm not going to stutter at all. I feel like I know what I need to tell him so he'll arrest Mr. Bowen and save Noah.

"Your dad goes to my church," I say.

"Saint Paul's?"

I nod. And lean into him. "Last week at church we were singing during Communion. One of my favorite songs. "As the Deer." Do you know it?"

He shakes his head.

"Well, your dad was there with this lady he sits with now. She's his friend. She's not your mom, right?"

He shakes his head again. He's looking really interested now. The other policeman clears his throat—code, I think, for 'Get her back on track' but Officer Bingham doesn't, so I keep going.

"They were really having wonderful worship time, this lady and your dad. I loved watching them. They had their eyes closed, and their arms up in the air. I felt so happy for them. I felt so happy that he has this sweet companion now that he can worship with." I feel like I'm going to start crying again. I'm not sure why. I'm probably just tired. But I take a breath and keep talking, even though it comes out all jittery. "Because I know he and . . . Mrs. Bingham loved to worship too."

He's frowning at me now like he can't figure out what I'm telling him.

"And then, out of nowhere, right there in church, in my head, I saw your dad—in my head. And he was running in this field . . . this really pretty field . . . and he was excited, so excited about wherever he was running. And then I saw your mom." I pause to gather myself. I want him to visualize what I saw. I have to calm down and be clear. "And she was in a wheelchair, like she was the last couple of years at church, before she died, I mean. And I realized that's who your dad was running to. And as he got closer to her, she stood up, just stood right up, easy as pie, and started running to him. When your dad reached your mom, he picked her up and twirled her around, like they were kids, you know? And they were so happy. *I knew they were in Heaven*. In my head, I knew it. And I knew, even though that moment hasn't happened for your dad yet, that it will."

I stop talking and remember how I felt, sitting in church, when I opened my eyes. I had no doubt. I knew I'd gotten a real glimpse . . . of Heaven.

Officer Bingham looks at me for a long time. The other police officer clears his throat for the second or third time.

"I get that you think I'm not right in the head. I'm telling you, for whatever reason, I see things, not always, but sometimes. I'm not making this up. I *saw* Mr. Bowen with Noah. I saw it the morning after Noah disappeared. I hear this crazy sound sometimes when I see things—like a ripping sound, like the sky is ripping. Mr. Bowen walked up to Noah, and he leaned over to say something to him, and they went away. *I saw it.* And on Halloween, I saw Noah's book bag in his house. The hand that I found under the bed is part of an action figure, and the rest of it was in his sweatshirt pocket, the one he had on the day he disappeared. It's a red sweatshirt. You guys found it, right? I know you did. You found it with his books."

"What?" he says, looking confused and like he suddenly doesn't trust me at all. The other cop looks stunned too.

"Noah must've had it—Anakin, I'm talking about Anakin—in his pocket, and it

fell out, just the hand I mean, when Mr. Bowen put him in that room, the guest room, to hide him or something. I don't know. Maybe he was holding the toy in the room or something, and the hand fell off. Or maybe he hoped it could be like Hansel and Gretel's bread crumbs. I don't know that part. I mean, I can't see it."

They're both watching me. But I can't tell what either one thinks.

"You know how sometimes you just know something is true?"

I'm so intent on being clear and speaking the words in my head that I don't even know I'm crying until Officer Bingham hands me a tissue.

"Someone has to believe me. This guy is a bad man. I know it. And maybe Noah's already dead, but I don't think Mr. Bowen is done taking kids."

Nobody says anything. I'm starting to think they're going to stick me in some dirty old jail cell, or a padded one, when Officer Bingham looks at the other guy and says, "See if they're a match." He looks at me. I don't say a word.

After the second police officer leaves, Officer Bingham says, "You'll appear before the Juvenile Master, Grace. He'll be very stern and disapproving, do you understand? Nobody wants a town full of fourteen-year-old girls who go breaking into neighbors' homes. Look sorry, okay?"

I nod.

"Then I'll go to Jason Bowen's house and inform him that his house was broken into." He's talking slowly now. "In order to ensure that the thief didn't take anything else, I'll insist on a thorough search of the premises. Grace, I'll insist on *a thorough search. Very.* And if anything at all is found, anything at all questionable . . ."

"So I'm spending the night in jail?"

"I doubt it. Just listen to the Juvenile Master. I expect he'll release you to your parents' custody. And then, Miss Sherlock Holmes, let us do our job. Nod your head, Grace, and tell me you understand me."

"I understand you," I say, nodding madly.

"Don't assume the police aren't following tips just because you don't see search parties. Remember that."

I'm being escorted out the door when Officer Bingham says, almost shyly, "Mom looked happy?"

"Ecstatic," I tell him, and mean it.

By the time the Juvenile Master is done talking to me, it's almost 3 a.m. When we get home, everybody's asleep. Mom and Dad don't say much. They both kiss me on the forehead at the bottom of the steps to my room. Nobody's mad at me.

"I didn't get to tell you," Dad says softly after Mom has gone into the bathroom. "I think you're a terrific actor. I mean, actress. I love you baby." And he hugs me.

I fall asleep surprisingly fast.

I hear running water. I can't see it yet. I know it's close, and I feel like I have to find it. I'm not sure if I'm hunter or hunted, but I'm in the woods, somewhere. It's familiar, somehow, these woods. The trees are gigantic, and thin, and there are lots of dead branches strewn across my path. They seem like they're leaning in to look at me. The knots in the bark have morphed into eyes. There are shadows here, too, hiding behind the trees. I start running, and I hear fluttering noises, like there's bats or owls in the trees. I'm afraid I'll get bitten by a bat, or something worse, and I start running faster. I hit something that's laying across the path and start falling. I turn around to see what tripped me.

"Ahhhhh!" My scream wakes me up, and I quickly roll onto my stomach and muffle the sound before I wake up the whole house. I look at the closest alarm clock. It's 6 a.m. I went to bed three hours ago. I sit up in bed and twist on a Christmas light. Did I dream that I tripped over Noah's body? Is that what I saw? I lie back down and think. I can't see it anymore. I close my eyes and try to bring it back. I know I've been in the woods I just dreamed about.

***

Clementine thinks about rabid animals and how they lash out when you corner them. That's what these demons remind her of, wild animals foaming at the mouth.

After he sees Grace running away and closes the window, Bowen paces back and forth in all the rooms, studying each one, and Clementine is glad, despite her terror, that Grace has so unhinged him. He walks into the guest room and reclines for a moment, head poised on the pillow, scanning the room, his eyes panning every surface. Satisfied he's safe, he answers the door when the police arrive. They speak of a break-in and apologize for the inconvenience of bothering Bowen so early this morning. They tell him the girl was released into her parents' custody and talk about a routine search just to make sure nothing else was taken. The man seems concerned by the word "else." But the police assure him the trinket she stole wasn't much and will be returned shortly, and they ask if he wants to press charges.

"Grace O'Shaunessy?" he asks. Clementine watches him flex his fingers behind his back. She smells his sweat. "Else" torments him. Good.

He tells them he won't press charges, and still they search. She realizes the police are stalling. She watches one look at the other. Bowen wants them to leave. One officer suggests Bowen sit down in the living room. Clementine can't abide the air in this house, so she slips outside. The stench of fear and hatred smells like a battlefield, like death. Outside, she watches Grace and her sister driving away.

"Save the boy," Clementine tells her.

Moments after the police leave, Clementine steps inside. Bowen sits on the sofa, staring down, thinking. Then he stands, and flanked by shadows on all sides, goes back into the guest room and kneels down on the floor. To pray? He picks up a long white feather, his hand shaking as he studies this remnant of the angel. He turns it over. It is translucent in the morning sun. And then it bursts into flame, scorching his fingers.

He falls backward, dropping what is no longer a feather at all. Flames lick the bedspread. He runs to the kitchen and fills a bucket with water. Then, before the whole house catches fire, he runs back to the room and douses the bed with water.

His fingers throb. He puts ice in a bowl and lays the reddened fingers within, leaning on the counter. He looks out the kitchen window and across the grass to Grace's house. Clementine watches his pupils dilate, but she can't read him. She can't read what's on his heart. His heart is buried— buried like an innocent victim at the bottom of a well.

Having numbed the pain, he leaves the house. She watches him walk across the street. When he finds out Grace is gone, he'll know she's gone to save the boy.

"Satan himself masquerades as an angel of light."
~ 2 Corinthians 11:14

Chapter 21

It's 9 a.m. on Saturday morning, and we're driving to Cunningham Falls, up the winding mountain road. My body feels all tingly again, but that could be due to lack of sleep and excessive caffeine.

"Okay, so you dreamed about Cunningham Falls. So what do we do? Just park up here and take the path to the Falls?"

I nod. Mary nods back.

I finally broke down and told Mary everything. When I woke up early this morning, I spent an hour figuring out who to beg for a ride. I thought about asking Julie to drive. But then I imagined how it would be if we found Noah's remains up here, how awful that would be for her. If it was my brother, I wouldn't want to be stuck with some terrible image in my head of my dead brother for the rest of my life.

So then I thought about anyone else I know who drives—Mom, Dad, Peter, even Hayden—but I had so many reasons not to ask this one or that one that I finally just broke down and woke up Mary. And the answer I got was no, along with a pillow thrown at me. I went outside and sat on the stone steps and stared at Mr. Bowen's house for a while. Then I went back up to our room. Bridget was still asleep, but Mary was up, painting her toenails and texting at the same time. I sat on her bed, ducking so I didn't hit my already bruised head on the top bunk, and whispered as softly as I could. I didn't want to wake up Bridget. I knew my chances of getting Mary to drive totally depended on not involving Bridget.

"I *really* need you to drive me to Cunningham Falls."

"No." She looked at me, raised her eyebrows and jutted out her chin—just to make sure I understood just how much she meant it—exhaled loudly, and responded to her latest text. After a moment, focused on her nails again, she said, "Why? I thought you were under house arrest or something."

"No, I'm not. I'm just not allowed to be on Mr. Bowen's property."

"I can't. I have too much homework. And Dad is dragging us all back to your show tonight." She looked up, aware I may have taken that last remark the wrong way. "You were great, but I already saw it, you know?" She paused. I didn't say anything. "Anyway . . ." And she read another text.

She stretched out her legs, forcing me off the bed. So I knelt on the floor and leaned across her bed. "Mary, Noah is being kept someplace near the Falls. If I don't find him *today*, he'll die. Mary? He will die. I absolutely know it. I absolutely know he's there, and I absolutely know this is our last chance to save him."

She looked up from her phone and spilled her Calico Red nail polish all over her white bedspread. "Crap!"

I got up and gave her a little space. "What the frick, Gracie!"

We took the bedspread to the basement and did as much damage control as we could before sticking it in the washing machine. Somehow, by the time we'd doused it with *Shout*, I'd talked her into driving.

As we pulled out onto the street, having taken Peter's car, I saw my white-haired friend. She was sitting on Mr. Bowen's back patio. When we saw each other, she stood up and said something. There were also three police cars there. I hoped by now Officer Bingham had told Mr. Bowen I was the one who broke in. Let him worry about whether I found something. I hoped those guys could keep Mr. Bowen busy.

We park on the road. There are lots of cars here. It's a beautiful day—mid-fifties—crazy-nice for November. We get out and follow a path that leads to the Falls, me first and Mary behind me. I stop as we arrive at the waterfall. Kids are climbing the rocks, and parents are taking pictures. There's a guy with a prosthetic leg climbing along on a slippery rock. Part of me wants to run up the mountain and help him get to wherever he's going, but Mary pulls me back to our purpose. I sit on a rock and try to concentrate. She sits too.

"Maybe I'm wrong," I say.

"What? Are you kidding me?"

"He *was* here. But . . ." The tingling is worse. I look around. I blink a few times, and the whole Falls is like one of those posters with embedded pictures that you can only see if you somehow look past the first picture. If I stare at one place long enough, a whole other picture emerges, like I'd ripped a canvas in half and discovered a second, richer layer of the same painting— more beautiful, more detailed, with brighter colors—and it had lay there hidden behind the first one. I see my white-haired lady, standing on a rock, maybe twenty feet from me. I look carefully and notice how young she is, maybe younger than me even, and she has huge, glistening wings. Huge. *She is an angel.* My white-haired friend is an angel. And I know her. I remember her. I named her. She was my imaginary friend. My mouth drops open.

"Clementine?"

"What?" Mary asks.

I look beyond Clementine and see,—a little less clearly, less vividly— more angels. I'm not sure how many. They're all over the place.

"Oh *God!*"

"What? Jesus, Gracie! What?"

I look back to my angel. She's shaking her head. She's telling me I'm not in the right place. Noah was here, but he's not now. Am I supposed to go someplace else? I stand up, feeling like maybe I'll faint now. But I don't. I walk closer to her. My entire body is totally electrified. I touch my hair and try to pat it back down. The closer I get, the worse it feels.

"Grace." She's smiling at me. She has this absolutely terrific smile. "You can do this, Grace. But there's so little time." I don't so much hear her voice with my ears as receive it inside myself, but it's her. I recognize her voice. And it's coming from the same place as the ripping noise.

"But I don't know where to go," I say out loud.

"What?" says Mary. "I thought you had a . . . vision. Gracie! I thought you saw him here. You said you saw him. You said you *absolutely* saw him. You said it twenty flipping times."

159

"He was," I whisper. I look up to the top of the Falls. There are all kinds of people there. I keep my eyes trained on a spot at the top, and wait.

In what almost looks like slow motion—or maybe that's just because I'm looking at something that already happened—I see Mr. Bowen with Noah, and another boy, too, an older boy I don't recognize. They're pointing at the rocks at the very top of the Falls and talking. Mr. Bowen wants them to climb on the rocks. The older boy seems willing enough, but Noah is shaking his head, pulling away. He looks scared. They turn and leave. They take a path that leads over the hill, and then I don't see them anymore.

"He's near here, Mary. We have to go back to the car and drive further up the mountain. He's near here." I'm not a hundred percent sure of that even as I say it, but something makes me say it.

Mary looks uncertain. I'm sure she's tired of this wild goose chase, but she probably figures at this point, she might as well see this to the end.

"Trust me," I say, trying to sound more confident than I feel.

So we go. We get back in the car and drive further up the mountain. My ears pop. We start descending down the other side. I see houses.

"Where?" she asks me.

I'm confused again. What am I doing? What the heck am I doing?

All these houses look safe, homey. Nothing seems like a place anyone would use to kidnap children. There are all kinds of Thanksgiving decorations on them. Then I see a house on the left side of the road that unfurls every red flag in my head.

"Mary! That's it. Pull in." She does.

I think about Peter's car sitting in this driveway. "Wait. We have to hide the car." She nods, pulls out, and drives further down the road. We park so the Buick is pretty much hidden by trees on the other side of the road, about a quarter of a mile away. Then we walk back.

We stand in front of the house, considering our situation. It's an old farmhouse-style house, painted yellow a long time ago and now peeling badly. There's a big detached garage, also yellow and peeling, with dirty contact paper covering up the windows. Why would anyone put contact paper over windows? There's an ancient-looking well in the front yard with

160

some missing stonework. And no decorations for Thanksgiving. Mary scans the windows. Everything looks dark inside except for a blue glow coming from one second story window— telltale sign of a TV on somewhere.

"Let's just knock," Mary says.

"Right," I agree. I think about the Juvenile Master and what he said about staying off Mr. Bowen's property. So if this house belongs to Mr. Bowen, too, and I'm on his property again—does that mean I'm breaking the law right now? Will I be laying my head down in Hagerstown tonight, or wherever the facility is for errant girls? Who will they get to play Helen tonight?

Mary knocks, and what sounds like a big dog starts barking inside. But nobody answers the door. My sister is flattening her curly mane against the stained glass windows that frame the front door. One of the windows has a few cracks, which is affording her some kind of a view of the inside. A black lab gallops down the stairs and keeps crazily barking on the other side of the glass.

I'm thinking we should investigate the backyard, but I don't want to leave Mary alone here, and I don't want to fly solo myself, either.

Her hands pressed against the glass to minimize glare, she says, "Someone's home. They're just not answering the door."

And then, out of the corner of my eye, I see a shadow in the upstairs window. By the time I look up, it's gone. I try staring at it, hoping it will materialize like my angel did at the Falls. No such luck.

"You want to check out the backyard?" Mary asks.

"Okay," I say, keeping the corner of my eye trained on that window. We walk around to the side of the house. There's a basement door like the kind in *The Wizard of Oz*—I think it's called a Bilco door. A rusted padlock lies open on the dirt next to it. Mary is ahead of me now, and I run to catch up. I look up to another window—probably the back side of the same room. A boy about my age is watching us. For a second, I'm scared. But then I think maybe he's not real, and I'm not sure I should tell Mary what I see . . . but then he opens the window.

"Are you looking for something?" The dog must've gone back upstairs because now its madcap barking is coming from the upstairs window.

"Do you live here?" Mary asks.

"Who wants to know?"

"We're lost," she says.

"What, in my backyard?" He seems pretty unfriendly and not at all buying our little ruse.

I'm busy watching the road, the yard, the other windows while Mary attempts to make a friend.

"We're looking for Jason Bowen," she says. "He teaches at Saint Anthony's, you know, in Thurmont. He's our brother's teacher."

"And?"

"Well, our brother owes him a paper. I have it . . ." She sticks her hand in her pocket and pulls out a flash drive. "Peter's sick. He has . . . the flu, so he couldn't bring it up."

The kid doesn't believe her. He's looking at her like he knows she's totally making this up, but he has to keep listening because he came to the window instead of ignoring us.

"Okay," he says. "Just put it through the mail slot. Write your name on it."

"So he lives here? This is Jason Bowen's house?"

"He's my dad."

Well, here's a crazy complication. Mr. Bowen has a son in Thurmont, but he lives alone in Butler. Is this the boy Caleb thought committed suicide? Shouldn't he be a lot older?

He leaves the window. He's probably on his way downstairs. Mary has the flash drive, and she's walking around to the front yard. I follow, but as I pass the basement, I grab the door handle and step inside. I'm almost in when Mary comes running back for me.

"Gracie, no!" she whispers and pulls the door all the way open to drag me out.

"Mary, I've got to check."

She moans and follows me.

The Bilco door slams shut above our heads, and we catch ourselves before we fall all the way down the cement steps that lead from the door to the dirt floor. It's so dark. Perched about halfway down, my sister curses at me and then pulls out her phone so she can see a little bit. Even with just the light of Mary's cell phone and thin blades of light sneaking under the door, I see all kinds of nooks and crannies down here. This house is probably two hundred years old, and the basement has a labyrinth of hallways.

"Well, that was stupid," whispers Mary.

"Not if Noah's here," I whisper back and pull her with me down to the floor.

And then, as if I conjured him by speaking his name, Noah walks around the corner from some back hallway. I'm speechless. He's here. We saved him. We'll get him out through this basement door and back home. Officer Bingham won't be mad at me that I broke my promise. I won't go to jail. Mr. Bowen will.

Then, some ice-cold spider of a crawler creeps up my spine, and I feel like my heart stopped beating. I realize the obvious. Mary doesn't see Noah. She *won't* see him because Noah—our Noah, our flesh and blood Noah—is dead. I'm looking at his spirit—the same spirit that's been trying to talk to me all fall. I want to tell God off so badly right now. I mean, really scream at Him. What was the point of all this? Noah's dead. So God, or God along with some band of angels, has led me on a scavenger hunt since September trying to save a dead boy's life. Why? To avenge him? What, am I Hamlet now? And as I stand here in this stunned, scared rage, this ghost of Noah is looking at me with this crazy look on his face, and again, I have no idea what he's trying to say. Mary is talking, or whispering, a blue streak, but Noah doesn't say a word. Poor Noah, who always had something to say, stands here silent.

"We have to get out of here. You're not supposed to set one foot on this guy's property, right? Come on!"

I look at her. She's looking at me. She doesn't see Noah. I'm the only one who does. I feel exhausted. My eyes are burning, and then tears start to flow. I want to grab him and hug him tight, and tell him how sorry I am that I didn't find him, but I'm afraid I'll embrace air, and then I'll lose it. And I want to know *when* he died. And *how*. I want him to tell me if Mr. Bowen killed him, and what he wants me to do about it. I'm drowning in a muddy, murky sea of questions and guilt. The only thing I do know is I see things other people don't see, and ultimately, it didn't make any difference at all.

"You're dead, right?" I whisper.

"What?" Mary asks, busy heading back up the steps, one hand holding her phone in front of her and the other hauling me. "No, we're not dead yet. Come on." Noah just nods.

Maybe if I'd gone out that first night, the night the angel told me to, I would've found him. But I stayed home in my safe house and did nothing. Maybe if I'd done something that first night, I could've saved Noah's life. That's probably when he died. That's the way it works.

"Grace, come on!" Mary pushes the door open. I'm watching Noah, not wanting to leave any part of him, even if it's his spirit part rather than his living body, standing here in this lonely place. What kind of a God would leave the spirit of a kid hanging out here in this dark basement? Why isn't Noah in Heaven? He shakes his head like he doesn't want me to leave.

I hear a car engine turn off. Mary and I look at each other. We implode. Moments later the front door opens. The dog starts barking again. Mary madly pushes me in front of her and out the door.

"Now!" she whispers furiously. Her eyes are popping out of her head. She's right. If it's Mr. Bowen who's here, and he realizes we're here, he'll kill us like he killed Noah. I force myself not to look back at him—at the spirit of this poor, murdered boy. Why would God abandon him here? I hold the door open for Mary, just a little bit, so Bowen and his son can't see us from a window, while she crawls out after me. She stops. We hear someone crying upstairs. The crying is mixed up with the din of barking. It's a familiar voice. At the same time, we register whose voice we recognize crying. Bowen took my little brother Sean.

"My God sent his angel, and he shut the mouths of the lions. They have not hurt me, because I was found innocent in his sight."
~ Daniel 6:22

Chapter 22

Mary sort of freefalls back down the steps, and I follow, trying to minimize the noise we make as the door slams shut again, and I fall on top of her. Noah is in the corner of the room now, pointing at some kind of crawl space behind him. Just where no sane girl would ever want to go. People are walking directly above us. Sean is still crying. The dog isn't barking anymore. I want to storm upstairs, grab my brother, and kill Bowen. I look on the ground for a weapon— a knife, a club, a bottle. But even as I imagine myself doing it, I know I can't. Bowen isn't a middle school bully, and we're not in a cafeteria. And when I fail, I won't get suspended. I'll die. And so will Mary and Sean. Mary is shaking all over.

"Mary, call 911."

She tries. "No service."

More walking. Noah is still beckoning me like crazy. I get down on my hands and knees and follow Noah. Past the crawl space, we find a sketchy closet. Noah gestures to me like I should climb inside.

"Let's hide," I whisper to Mary. "Let's hide and figure out how to get Sean out of here."

"That boy we talked to knows we're here," Mary whispers back, shaking her red head and looking in the direction of the stairs. "He must!"

"Well, what do you want to do? Leave Sean?"

"No!"

"So we hide. Mary, come on." It's not that I'm feeling in charge or calm or anything like that. I just know that if Mary and I both lose it, we're all dead.

I follow Noah into the recesses of the closet, and Mary follows me. It's way darker the further we get from the Bilco door and daylight. We settle into the closet and tuck in our body parts and each other, close.

"We've got to get Sean without him seeing us," Mary whispers into my ear.

"Right."

I want to tell her I don't think we have much time—that I think Mr. Bowen killed Noah the night he took him. I don't, though. I just agree with her. Of course, we can't let him see us. He'll kill us all.

I mull over a possible chain of events. If the police told Bowen I broke into his house, and he didn't press charges, then I guess the police weren't allowed to snoop around his whole house. That would've been smart on his part. But I got the feeling from Officer Bingham they were going to search his house whether he wanted them to or not. Couldn't they strongly suggest they search just to protect him from this terrible teenage thief? Having never gotten arrested before, I don't know how it works. But when Mary and I left this morning, the police were at his house. So if the police were at his house, they must have searched, at least a little bit. But they didn't find anything. If they found something, Bowen would be in jail. So they left, and he went across the street and kidnapped my brother. That part is a real speed bump in the whole story. Why would he be so dumb? Wouldn't *he* think that was dumb? In a house full of people, how could he get away with that? It seems so twisted to kidnap my brother when he already knows I'm on to him— actually, it seems stupid.

But none of that matters, because Sean is here, and so is Mary. I walked all three of us into this.

Then the basement door opens, someone flips a light switch, and a single light bulb glows in the rafters somewhere. Heavy footsteps are walking down the stairs. The light bleeds into the closet enough to let me see how terrified my sister looks, just waiting for Bowen to find us. Noah sits in the corner on the other side of the closet. He looks scared too. He doesn't take his eyes off me. The dog is with whomever is coming. I know because, first, I hear the tap-tap-tap of paws, and then it starts barking again. The dog knows we're down here. I hear Bowen's voice from around the corner. He sounds close. Mary and I don't move a muscle. Noah is still looking at me like he's trying to communicate in spirit-talk. The dog comes around the corner, smells us I guess, and starts barking like crazy.

"Bess!" Mr. Bowen says in this voice I've never heard him use—this mean, low voice, like nothing in the whole world is funny at all. My whole body starts shivering, and then he opens the closet door where we're hiding.

"Greetings, ladies," he says in that same low gravelly voice that he just used with his dog. "I don't recall inviting you, but . . ." He shrugs. "Ahh, what the hell, right?" He smells like alcohol.

Mary grabs my arm and squeezes, tight. I don't even try to talk because I know I don't have any words. It's like I can almost feel the air taking my words away, just scooping them up, and I'm left mute, like Helen.

"I hate to disappoint you, but the lad you seek is . . . indisposed."

Then he drags us out—me first, and then Mary. For a second, I think he's going to dive in again and grab Noah, but when I look back, Noah's gone. Bowen's saying something to us, but the whole nightmare is turning into some kind of silent movie. It's like I can't hear, or I can't hear him anyway. Instead, I hear wind and a kind of ringing noise, almost like wind chimes on someone's porch during a tornado. I look over at Mary. She's not standing next to me anymore, where she just was. He must've shoved her, or she fell, because now she's in a corner a few feet away, and I can see she's screaming something at me. Maybe it's my name. But I can't hear words. Mary is looking at something past me, so I turn around too. And there's Bowen, and he has a gun, and I guess he's aiming it at me.

I fall backward, trying to get away from him, trying to bury myself in some dark corner of this basement so he doesn't shoot me. My head smacks into the cinderblock wall, and for a second I think maybe I'll just go to sleep, and it will all be over. I want to cover Mary with my body so at least he won't shoot her, too, but she's too far away. I close my eyes, and I start to float someplace else, someplace better.

But then, the weirdest thing of all happens. Some kind of crazy bright light makes me open my eyes again, I mean *bright* light, not like light bulb light, or even daylight. *And I see angels.* They're big, huge, and *not* children at all. They're nothing like I ever imagined. They're so bright the whole basement lights up, and they take up all the space. They look like warrior angels, but not the way I always imagined Gabriel would look when he was protecting the baby Jesus—more like guerilla warfare angels, like if they had on camouflage, the picture would be complete. They have swords, big ones. They look furious too. I think about the whimsical little smiles on the stained glass angels at church. These guys look nothing like them—and these angels are everywhere. The bad shadows are here, too, except they look more solid than they ever did in my dreams—and a lot more disgusting. They're some awful mash-up experiment of alligators and burn victims, and they have some kind of lethal-looking weaponry too—more like daggers and switchblades than majestic swords. I remember the shadows from my dreams, the pockets of darkness that seep around corners, whistling and breathing and making everything feel cold and wet. These are worse because they're so close I can touch them. And they're real. I don't want to look at them, but I can't help it. They're just too freaky looking. I look at Bowen, and he's not pointing his gun at me anymore. He looks like he's losing his balance or something, and he's yelling at us instead, like he thinks it's our fault his basement floor has started tilting and shaking—which, by the way, it is . . . tilting and shaking, I mean. It's like an earthquake is happening down here.

Angels are fighting monsters everywhere, and unlike us humans, they don't seem deterred by the shaking ground or horrific noise.

I see Mary crawl around the corner and head for the stairs. I try to make him look at me instead of her, hoping she'll find Sean upstairs, and they'll get away.

"Hey!" I say, and he drops his gun, trying to keep from falling down. He lunges at me and grabs my hair, and a great big angel grabs him. I see the angel. I'm inches from his face. He's big and strong. He's a man, an angry man, and except for the fact that he's glowing and has wings, he looks as solid as me. Weirder, I can tell by Bowen's reaction when the angel grabs him that Bowen *doesn't* see him. He's just madder, thinking somehow I pulled away from him on my own, that I'm that strong. He wraps his arm around me and hugs me around the waist so hard it feels like he just squeezed out all my air, and kneels down, taking me with him, and picks up his gun. He digs the barrel into my head, right next to my eyebrow. It's totally loud down here with all the ringing noises and the wind and the crazy dog barking at all the angels and monsters. I start talking to him—Mr. Bowen, I mean—really fast, which I know is dumb, because all he has to do is pull the trigger, and the last thing I should want to do is tick him off. But I can't stop myself. All the words that got sucked out of me a few minutes ago leaped back in and won't hush.

"I know about your son—I don't mean the boy upstairs, who probably isn't even your son."

He screams something, probably "shut up", but I can't hear him.

"I know you killed Noah too. And now you want to kill me. But I think the person you really want to kill is yourself."

I'm crying now, but it's not because I'm scared. I don't feel particularly scared of Bowen anymore, or of death even. I'm crying because it's all so wrong. All around us in this basement, angels and what I can only guess are demons are battling it out. I see and hear swords crashing into each other. And Bowen has no idea. He doesn't see any of it. What are they fighting for? His soul? Is that what's happening here?

"You can stop. You don't have to keep doing this. Something evil has a noose wrapped around your neck. You're the only one who can take it off."

I have no idea what's compelling me to say these words, but as I speak them I know they're true.

"God never stopped loving you," I say, kind of hyperventilating and screaming at the same time. I feel the gun being pulled away, and at first I think it's over, that he knows he did wrong and all that, and we're safe. He backs away from me, his lips all quivery, his permed hair standing on end. He looks like he just stuck his finger in an electric socket. And then I see his gun—he's clutching it like it's a baseball. He's the pitcher, and I'm the unlucky batter. I feel something hard smack me on the top of the head.

I close my eyes. This must be it. This is when I'll pass out, or die. But ridiculously, my eyes flutter open again. I feel like Rocky in the ring with Apollo Creed—no matter how many times he tries to knock me out, I rally.

Bowen crawls across the floor. He looks like somebody who's trying to escape from a burning building. He's keeping his body close to the ground and covering the bottom part of his face with his flannel shirt, like you would if you were crawling out of a house on fire. He's trying not to suffocate from smoke, even while he's coughing and screaming things at me. But I can still tell he can't see the battle. Demons are using their claws to shred angels' wings. The angels are screaming something as they lunge and slice with their huge, gleaming blades. I try to focus on what's coming from their mouths. I can't separate the sound they're making from the cacophony of noises bouncing off the walls down here.

I make myself rise from where I'm sprawled out on the ground and kneel. I crawl closer to the angels. They're praising God.

"Hallelujah! Salvation and glory and power belong to our God, for true and just are his judgments."

They're staving off the demons with praise. I'm awestruck, paralyzed by the realization that I'm actually seeing this while kneeling here on the dirt in this forgotten basement in the Catoctin Mountains. Their gorgeous and huge swords, glimmering with lethal glory, are more the prop than the predator. It's their *praise* that's beating these demons.

"Hallelujah! For our Lord God Almighty reigns. Let us rejoice and be glad and give him glory! Hallelujah!"

"Hallelujah!" I say, loud enough to hear myself above the din. "Hallelujah!" I say again. My whole body shivers with energy.

A demon crouching near me—it looks sort of like a cross between some kind of wild boar and gigantic frog—eases away from me. The demons try writhing past the angels to separate the angels from Bowen. But as more moments pass and the angels keep worshipping louder and louder, more of the demons turn into vapor—they look more like the shadows I see in my dreams than the monsters with claws they were before. I can see now that they aren't *protecting* Bowen—the demons aren't his guardians. They're imprisoning him.

Clementine sits beside me. I'm utterly safe. Warm tears stream down my cheeks. I wrap my arms around her. She's solid, and bigger than I remember.

Bowen seems crazed. He's gotten to the stairs, his dog by his side, and he keeps almost gaining, and then losing, his balance. Three angels flank him. I don't understand why, but I think the demons' desire tonight was to destroy Bowen—right now. Like tonight Satan could use him to do some really awful things, and then kick him to the curb of eternity. But God hasn't given up on him, so He sent his angels to fight for Bowen. But he can't see any of it.

He opens the door to the upstairs. Mary and I have to get upstairs, too, so we can find Sean and escape. I want to. I want to bolt up the stairs, but I know I'm bleeding where Bowen hit me with his gun, and I have no more strength.

I look for Mary. At first I don't see her. She's not where she was. She's not on the stairs. I think maybe she got away. Maybe while Bowen was down here, she and Sean got away. But then I do see her. She's lying on the ground near the stairs, crumpled up. She's not moving. I want to call her, run to her, wake her up. But even as I'm trying to sit up, the protection of Clementine's wings makes me so sleepy. It's quiet again, and I close my eyes and let it be over.

***

While warriors battle all around her, Clementine sees Bowen strike Grace and runs to her. Enraged, she assaults him. Her strikes send him reeling. His arms and neck collide with the wall, and he lands on the dirt floor just a few feet from Grace. Clementine kneels beside Grace and leans down to her. She kisses her forehead. Grace breathes.

"It's not your time," Clementine cries, not sure if this is true.

Then she picks the girl up, cradles her, and carries her away from the battle.

And she goes to encourage the boy.

She finds him hidden in his room, under the covers. His heart is more transparent than Bowen's, but he's still much harder to read than Grace. Sorrow hides his heart from Clementine. Years of loneliness built armor no child should need to wear.

She climbs under his blanket inside the tent he's created. "You can save another boy," she says. She gently takes his chin in her white hands—hands more solid than they were two months ago, so much more solid than Clementine herself realizes—and she crouches down to see his face. "A boy just like you were."

She waits beside him. She watches him fight his worst fear. Then, after a long time, he slowly lifts his head from beneath the scratchy gray army blanket. He bunches it up and tosses it onto the bed. And walks out of the room.

171

*"Mounted on a mighty angelic being, he flew, soaring on the wings
of the wind."*
~ 2nd Samuel 22:11

Chapter 23

I wake up, and even before I open my eyes I know the angels are gone. And, thank God, the demons too. Wherever I am now, it's absolutely dark. I sit up. Aside from an awful headache, I seem to be okay. It's really pitch dark now. It must be late. I remember my play. I missed my closing night.

I hear Mary's voice, and once I get my bearings, I crawl toward it. I was in another of these crazy little nooks that are all over this ancient basement. I stop when I hear an unfamiliar guy's voice answer her.

"Shouldn't have come here," he says, or something like that.

"Where's Sean?" Mary asks.

They're both whispering, but I can hear them well, so I must be just around the corner. I wait to hear what the other voice says. Nothing.

"Tell me."

Then the guy starts to cry. I can tell he's young—it's definitely not Bowen's voice.

"Tell me," Mary says again, and then she's crying too.

"I can't. He'll be mad."

"So what are you doing here?"

"I was just . . . I . . . I thought you were dead . . . I'm sorry. You shouldn't have come here. Why'd you . . ."

I crawl around the corner, and there sits Bowen's son.

"Gracie!" Mary starts inching toward me. Her clothes are dirty, and her face looks like she got scratched. "I thought you . . ." and that's it for Mary. She starts bawling.

I look at the boy, who's backing away from us.

"Where's Sean?" I ask him.

I don't read anything bad inside this kid—just grief, miles of it. He doesn't answer, but he doesn't look away, either. We look at each other, and it hits me that he was the kid by the stream. I recognize his eyes—I remember this same expression in his eyes. Bowen must've been in the car along the highway that night, waiting. This boy must've dumped Noah's stuff in the woods. I guess he was the other person in Bowen's house too.

"You're his son?" I ask. It's just not right. This kid is my age.

He nods. "I thought you were dead," he says. "I thought my dad . . ."

"Where's our brother?" I ask.

Then the boy backs away from us and runs up the stairs.

Mary and I tiptoe up the basement stairs and try to turn the knob. Locked. We try to find our way back to the Bilco door. It takes a while. I keep listening, hoping the boy will come back downstairs—or that Noah will show up to lead us out of here. Finally, Mary sees the closet we hid inside when we first got here, and then we retrace our steps from there to the Bilco door. I climb the five cement steps and try to soundlessly push open the heavy door. Also locked. I remember the rusted padlock that was lying in the dirt. I should've taken it when I could.

So Mary and I sit down on the bottom step. We wrap our arms around each other, and we wait. At some point she starts humming worship songs in my ear—very out of character for my sister—and I start breathing a little easier. I try to block out images of Bowen hurting Sean. I pray.

About an hour passes, I guess, and the Bilco door opens. We both stifle small screams. But then we see Sean, crouching down with the twilight sky behind him, and he's holding the door open for us, madly waving his arm for us to move.

"Sean!" Mary says.

Noah, standing behind him, speaks directly to me. "Now!" he says. "Run!"

Words. Noah spoke words. Mary and Sean didn't hear him, but I did. Kind of like the same way I hear Clementine's voice. And the tone of it sounds like he's going to explode. So that's where Noah's been. With Sean. He's been taking care of Sean.

I creep up the steps as soundlessly as I can. Mary follows, almost knocking me over in her desire to get out of here.

It's pretty dark out. We stay hidden behind some bushes along the side of the house, trying to figure out what to do. Mary crawls along the grass, and Sean and I follow her. I look for Noah, but he's gone.

My thought is we'll stay low to the ground until we get to the other side of the road where the woods are, and then run. But Mary panics, and she doesn't wait that long. She bolts halfway across the front yard. So Sean and I run after her. We run across the road, and just as we reach the other side, the front door flies open, and Bowen sprints after us. Behind him is his son. He must have gone down to check on us in the basement right away, or maybe he saw us through the window. Or maybe he caught his son freeing Sean. We run without stopping and don't look back. The woods are dense and would provide a lot of cover except we're breathing hard and making lots of noise. He must be able to see us, and, I guess, catch us. The big thing we have in our favor is terror. That's giving us lots of adrenaline. There are no cars on the road now. All the visitors at the Falls have gone home. We run hard, but we're slowed down by these big rocks that are jutting out all over the place. Plus, there's a stream running madly below us—it's a big rocky drop, and the sound of it reminds me that if we lose our bearings and fall, we'll go flying into the water. And we're not running on level ground. But then, neither is he. I can hear him behind us. But not so close. Peter's car sits about a hundred yards ahead. We all three jump in and lock the doors. Mary starts the engine and turns the car around. She backs up too far, and I think we're going to go careening over the boulders and down into the water, but she shifts into drive in time, and we go flying back down the road, complete with squealing tires and gravel flying, just like a bona fide *Mission Impossible* episode. I look at the digital clock on the dashboard. 5:45. I try to figure out how long we were inside that house.

Mary has her eyes on the road, but I'm looking for Bowen. I don't see him. Or his son. Or Noah.

Sean curls up in the backseat.

Nobody speaks until we're well past the house and heading back down the mountain.

"Sean," I say, "are you okay?" He doesn't answer, and it hits me that he hasn't talked at all since we escaped.

"Sean?" Mary says, looking at him in the rearview mirror.

We drive for a while and stay quiet until Mary says, "I'm out of gas."

"Do we have money?" I ask.

"No."

We're still about a half hour from home, and if Bowen is following us, the gas gauge looks like we'll be on empty before we get back to Butler. I try Mary's phone. Still no service.

"Noah's dead," I finally say, breaking the silence. Mary and Sean both look at me.

"Did you . . ." Mary starts to say.

"I didn't see . . . his body," I say. "But he is, you guys. I know it."

We're quiet again. They know it too. You don't need a sixth sense to figure that out. Then I see, before I hear, Sean crying in the backseat. His shoulders heave up and down without making a sound. That's how my dad cries, too, soundlessly. I take off my seat belt and start climbing into the back with him.

"Gracie, stop. What are you doing?" Mary says when half of me has reached the backseat.

Now I'm next to him. I wrap him in my arms and cry with him. We cry for a while—for Noah, and maybe for ourselves, too, relieved that we're not all dead. I don't know how Bowen managed to grab my brother, but Sean's got dark circles under his eyes, and his whole countenance seems altered somehow. Bowen stole something from him today, maybe not physically— maybe he didn't have enough time to actually molest my brother—but he planted enough of a seed in Sean's mind that stole whatever innocence my brother had left. I think about the friends battling at the bus stop two months ago. I hold Sean tighter.

The phone beeps, alerting us we have service. We must be off the mountain. We can call the police.

"Call." Mary says.

I call Mom first. She must be flipping out by now. She picks up after half a ring.

"Mary?" Mom's voice screams into my ear.

"Mom."

"Grace? Where are you?"

"I'm with Mary. We have Sean. Mom, call Officer Bingham. Mr. Bowen is following us, and we're out of gas. Mom?"

The service is scratchy and awful.

"Gracie? Gracie?"

"Mom!" Call the police. We're in Peter's car. Mom!"

Then I lose her.

"There he is," Mary says. Sean and I turn around. She's right. Bowen's behind us.

***

The boy runs. At first, he follows Bowen. Clementine runs too. And then, as if he has actually sprouted wings of his own, Keith turns and runs the other way. And never looks back. Clementine stays with him until the police car stops. Until she knows he is finally safe.

"The best way out is always through"
~ Helen Keller

Chapter 24

Mary presses her foot down on the gas. I didn't think the Buick could go this fast.

For a split second, I think we'll get in trouble for speeding—and immediately realize that would be terrific.

"Maybe it goes longer than we think. Maybe it looks empty before it is," I say, leaning forward in the backseat and looking at the dashboard.

Bowen is still behind us, but we're not the only cars on the road, so he can't exactly drive at 100 mph and ram into us—another image from the movies. Well, I guess he could. But so far, he hasn't done that.

"Let's go to the show," Mary says.

"What?"

"Look." Butler High School is just beyond the traffic light. The light turns green, and now we're kind of coasting on an entirely empty tank of gas. Talk about angelic intervention. "Gracie, let's get inside. We'll be safer in the school. This car won't make it to the police station. It's still five miles from here."

We arrive in the school parking lot at 6:30. We look for his car, but we don't see him.

Once inside, Mary takes Sean to the cafeteria to try to call the police again. The service isn't great in the school, either. I think that's a plot to keep kids from texting, but it's a little better in the cafeteria, I guess because of all the windows.

I run to the drama wing. I'd totally forgotten about closing night. Actually, I guess I thought I'd be dead by now. Most of the cast is putting on makeup and getting hair done in the drama room. Music is playing. Some kids are singing along, and a few are dancing. I feel like I'm in *The Twilight Zone.* Lisa and Marty are in the hall as I walk past to go into Ms. D's room.

They're in the middle of some intense heart to heart. He's stroking her hair, and she's half-laughing, half-crying about something he's saying she must've misinterpreted.

"Call was at six," he says.

"He cheats on you nonstop," I tell Lisa and keep walking.

I grab a corner and mirror, shed my sweatshirt, pull my hair back, and go to work on myself. It doesn't take me long. I'm playing a little girl, so I don't need bunches of eye stuff—just enough so the stage lights don't wash me out. What I really need is time to find Helen. I can't imagine how I can do this. But here I am. Glimpses of today keep creeping across my mind's eye. I don't want them here—not now.

"Hey Grace, why didn't you go out with everybody for pizza last night?" says Caroline as she settles down next to me and concentrates on her eyeliner in my mirror.

"You disappeared after the show. Everybody was looking for you."

I remember leaping out the dressing room window, finding Anakin's hand. I thought I'd find Noah. I look at Caroline.

"Tired."

"Me too," she says. "And I don't have to do what you and Lisa do. But I slept in today. How about you?"

I shrug.

Lisa is now in costume, brushing her hair back into a bun, looking at me in the mirror. Caroline leans in closer.

"Lisa and Marty had a big fight at the pizza place," she whispers.

"Yeah?" I say. Boy, I don't want to hear about this.

"He's a player, you know? He just is. Lisa should understand that. He's been like this all the years I've known him. I mean, you don't really know him since you're just a freshman, but Grace, he just loves the attention. Maybe he's feeling unappreciated backstage. Wait 'til *Les Miz.*"

I must look confused.

"Ms. D picked the spring show. We're doing *Les Miserables.*"

"Wow," I say. But I don't know anything about it.

Then Caroline leaves me to myself, and I finish my face. I find Helen's jumper and go to the girls' dressing room. In costume, I find my way backstage. It's pretty empty. Most kids are still milling around the drama room. Since it's closing night, we'll probably have extra festivities. I nestle into a chair, lean my head back, and close my eyes. I imagine myself a six-year-old. I imagine my "mama" with her soft skin and silky hair, always giving me treats and kisses. I imagine the safety of her. I imagine the familiar things Helen feels every day—all the furniture, each piece in its proper place, her dog with his long fur, the food she finds on anybody's plates, hers for the asking. But overtaking these images, I see the long winding road up the mountain to Mr. Bowen's house in Thurmont, the huge rocks and running stream so close to the road, the trees, so tall and thin, leaning in as if to catch me. I see Noah's face and imagine his fear when he knew Mr. Bowen was going to kill him. I imagine what might've been happening to Sean all those hours when he was upstairs with Mr. Bowen. I see angels and demons fighting for us. I take a deep breath. What a crowded mess.

"Cast and crew—drama room—now," Marty whispers as he moves through the backstage space. I sneak a peek under the stage curtain. I see Mary and Sean. I don't see the rest of my family.

Back in the drama room, cast and crew are holding hands in a big circle. A senior is saying the closing night prayer. Ms. D is sniffling a bit, as are most of the seniors. I sneak in between Leo and Caroline. After the prayer, Ms. D hands out handwritten notes to everyone. When she gives me mine, I put it in my jumper pocket. This will be a special present for later. Marty calls "places", and we go to work.

During the first part of the show, when I'm "wild" Helen, it's easy to forget myself. I release myself to Helen's tantrums. I spend all my energy kicking Lisa, moaning, running into things, punching everything in my wake.

The really awful thing happens at the end of Act One. It's the scene when I drop the key—the key Helen used to lock Annie in her room. I drop it into the well. I'm onstage by myself with the key—or so Helen thinks. Annie is on stage, too, watching her. But Helen is sure she's alone. So I take the key out of my mouth, and I think about where I can put it where nobody will ever find it. I'm thinking about it, as Helen, and all of a sudden, in my head, I see Mr. Bowen thinking about where to put the key too—except in his case, the key is Noah's broken body. And just as Helen discovers the perfect spot for a disappearing act, so does, or did, Mr. Bowen—his well.

That's what he did with Noah. Shaking, Helen tosses the key down the well. I stand there while the lights go down and the curtain closes for intermission. I remember the well in his front yard, the stone well, probably two hundred years old, like his house.

I have to tell Officer Bingham. I can text him. He gave me his phone number at the police station last night. I run offstage and see Ms. D talking to Lisa.

"Excellent work," Ms. D says. "Keep remembering to face out in Act Two when it's just you and Grace for so long."

Then she sees me coming and lassoes me into their conversation. I do a little nodding, thinking about how I can make a break to find that phone number and a phone. The difference between Act One and Act Two, the two of them are saying, at least for Lisa and me, is that neither of us really gets any time offstage in Act Two. I use that segue to excuse myself to hit the bathroom, and then rush into the drama room to borrow a phone and grab the card Officer Bingham gave me at 2 a.m. Zach loans me his phone.

I want to make sure Mary and Sean are okay, so I crouch down to locate them under the stage curtain first. No one is sitting where they were sitting before the show started. I scan the auditorium. Pearl is talking to a boy I've never seen before. I see Bridget, or I should say, I see her hair, which *leads* me to see Bridget. She's standing in an aisle with my brother Shea, talking to someone who is sitting down. She throws her arms out, telling some story, and I see past her. Caleb. She's talking to Caleb. Caleb came to my play. Momentarily derailed, I watch him. Then I spot Mary, walking toward Bridget. Behind her I see Officer Bingham, Sean, and my parents. They're in the back. By their body language, I can tell they know at least some of what happened to Sean, what happened to all of us.

Mom has her arms around him, and Sean's not shooing her away like he usually does. My dad has his arm wrapped around Mary's shoulders, and as

I watch them, Dad takes a hanky out of his pocket and stops with her, right there in the aisle, and wipes her eyes for her. She tips her head down and rests it on Dad's chest. Sean wraps his arms around Mom. Dad kisses the top of Mom's head. I love them. I love them all.

The lights flash to tell the audience the second act is about to start.

"Noah's body in Bowen's well in Thurmont. Grace," I type into Zach's phone. I push "Send." Miraculously, it does.

I wait. I watch him feel for his phone and look at it. He pushes a button and reads. He just stands there for a second and then looks toward the stage. If I didn't know better, I'd say he's looking right at me. Then he comes jogging down the aisle. Everybody else is sitting down, and Officer Bingham is walking out the side door. Moments later, while I'm still on my tummy peeking through the bottom of the curtain, Mr. Bowen enters the auditorium from the back door, right where my parents and Sean were just standing. He just walks in. He has his hands in his pockets, and he looks awful. He looks like a hardcore alcoholic who just woke up after the bender to beat all benders. His hair is still sticking up, and even from across the auditorium, I can see his skin is all blotchy and sweaty. Nobody notices.

"M-m-m . . ." I whisper to no one, panic rising in my throat.

"Places," Marty is saying. "Grace, get the doll. It's still on the prop table. And don't do that. It's unprofessional." At first, I think he means the noise I'm making inside my throat. Then, I realize he thinks I'm sneaking a peek at the crowd.

"M-m-m . . ." I'm a motor, a useless motor. I'll either throw up, cry, or explode.

"Two minutes 'til curtain."

Officer Bingham arrives backstage. So does Lisa. I peek again. Mary and Sean sit, and Officer Bingham's partner sits next to them. He's looking around. I don't see Mr. Bowen now. Where'd he go? For whatever crazy reason, not seeing him, even though he's clearly lurking somewhere nearby, serves to unlock my words.

Standing up, I whisper to Officer Bingham, "Bowen's here. He just walked in."

"Places!" Marty whispers a final time. He looks at Officer Bingham like he's embarrassed to tell a police officer to beat it, but finally says, "Is there a problem here?" in a tentative, very un-Marty way.

"What's this about a well?" asks Officer Bingham.

"I saw it in my head," I whisper-speak, all my words cascading on top of each other. "Noah's body is in a well in Thurmont. In the mountains. Past Cunningham Falls. It's a big yellow farmhouse. And there's a kid there. He said Bowen is his dad. But I don't think he is. And Bowen's here. Now. We should stop the show." I whisper all this really quietly, so Marty can't hear me, which seems to irk him.

"Grace," Officer Bingham says, leaning close to me. "For right now, we should keep the show going. Bowen should think we don't know he's here. Can you do that?"

I nod.

"This stage is probably the safest place to keep you while we surround him. Okay?"

"Um, places," Marty says.

I grab the doll, Officer Bingham walks back out the stage door, and the curtain opens.

"Knowledge is love and light and vision."
~ Helen Keller

Chapter 25

Lisa and Caroline are playing scene one. I'm in this scene, too, by myself on the bed, sewing. I'm spotting the edge of the red EXIT sign, the one in the balcony. When I spot something that doesn't move, that helps me to let my eyes relax so they don't dart around and look at things the way a sighted person does. I noticed that a lot this fall when I was practicing being blind—if I don't have something to look at, my eyes stop focusing on things. Anyway, I like spotting just the edge of the EXIT sign. That much light doesn't blind me, I mean for real, but it helps me keep my eyes from looking at things. I keep seeing flickers of white light around the edges of the red. I focus on the white light for a moment—I'm trying to figure out what it is, a little worried the white light is a precursor to me passing out, from exhaustion, hunger, fear, you name it.

Then I see Bowen. He's in the balcony. He's leaning on the balcony railing and reeling a little like he lost his equilibrium. We don't sell tickets for balcony seats. The whole section is closed. What's he going to do, shoot me like he's John Wilkes Booth? How did he even get up there?

Lisa grabs my sewing card, and I'm supposed to jab her with my needle—not for real of course, but it needs to look like I really do. I'm so distracted by John Wilkes in the balcony that I do jab her. Annie always gasps when I pretend to jab her. Tonight, Lisa gasps louder than usual and sounds distinctly irritated. I'll hear about this later. Not now, though, because now we're into the dining room scene.

The whole "time loss" thing happens—even tonight, even with Bowen in the balcony. Lisa and I are one—we're two parts of a jigsaw puzzle with insanely jagged edges, and beyond all reason, we're a perfect match. She's locking the rest of the Kellers out of the dining room. I kick her, and she slaps me. I slap her back, or try to, and she slaps me again, harder than usual—payback, I guess. I'm not sure if it's the jab or the comment about her slimy boyfriend that made her mad. And so it goes. I throw spoon after spoon,

185

refusing to use utensils. One flies into the audience, and more flashes of white light glint off the stainless steel.

She gets a spoonful of cheerios and carrots into my mouth. I spit it out, and she douses me with a pitcher of water. Soaked, I open my mouth, and she shoves more food in. "G-o-o-d-G-i-r-l," she fingerspells. Then I pull her hair. It all comes cascading out of her bun, and the two of us wrestle under the table as the lights go down.

Expecting her to complain that I really jabbed her, I'm stunned when she gives me a hug under the table and whispers, "What a ride, Grace."

A moment later, after Marty has roughly dried me off with a big towel, I ask him if I can use his phone.

"What?"

"Really fast."

I text Officer Bingham to tell him I saw Bowen in the balcony, and then I'm onstage again.

I get a few pages off until the end of scene five when Annie and Helen go to the garden house. I crawl over by the curtain and peek out from the bottom. I see Sean and Mary, then the rest of the family. I try to see into the balcony, but it's too weird an angle from here. I have to assume Officer Bingham got my text, and everything is okay. I scoot out to the hallway to get a drink of water. Leaning over to get a drink, I see movement reflected in the water fountain. I stop and look around. Nobody's here, at least nobody I see. But I have chills shooting from the back of my neck down my back, and I feel like someone's watching me. What the heck am I doing out here *alone*?

Then I see Bowen. He's coming around the corner, way down the hall. The closest door away from him would take me backstage, but that would mean I'd have to walk in his direction. And he's walking fast. So I back up, thinking I'll run around the other side of the auditorium and go backstage that way. He gets closer, looking royally pissed off.

"You left without saying goodbye," he says, loudly—considering there's a show going on—and pulls something out of his pocket. Even before I see it, I know it's the gun he slammed me with a couple of hours ago.

Then I collide with someone else, and Bowen stops. I turn around. Hayden has his hairy arms wrapped around me.

"Whoa, G-g-gracie."

"Yeah, whoa, G-g-gracie," Bowen echoes, and shoots.

He pulls the trigger at exactly the same moment Marty opens the backstage door. Marty starts to say my name, but his voice gets swallowed by a gunshot. I guess Bowen got distracted when the door flew open, or maybe he's still recuperating from the battle in his basement that he couldn't see, because he misses me. And Hayden falls.

That's when everything shifts into underwater slow motion—but not like the sky is ripping open, or like I'm seeing an afterimage of a past event. I'm present—I'm seeing real time. I'm just . . . horrified.

After Bowen shoots Hayden, he hesitates—I guess he's confused that the wrong person went down. That moment of hesitation creates the tiniest vacuum—enough time for me to scream, and then Marty screams, and we're loud. Our screams must snap him out of his momentary pause because he runs. He could've gone on an insane shooting spree. But instead, he backs off and bolts. I can't tell where Hayden got shot, but he's bleeding from inside his shirt, a lot. I kneel next to him and cradle his head in my lap. I hear someone inside the auditorium telling everyone to remain seated, which never works out well. Voices get louder in there, and then people start screaming.

"Hey," I say, leaning close.

"G-g-gra," Hayden says, sounding surprised and woozy.

"I'm sorry," I say.

"Not your fault."

People run backstage. Somebody calls an ambulance.

"Son, are your parents here?" a teacher asks. And I remember Hayden, all alone in the emergency room with his finger sliced in half.

"Son?"

But he's not talking anymore.

"His last name is Satalino. He lives on Eaton Road," I say.

My family comes backstage. Dad sits next to me on the floor, out of breath. He looks relieved to see me.

"It's going to be okay," he says. "I think they already caught Bowen."

Before long, the back hallway is full of people, like last night. But it's not like last night at all. I wish I could make the hallway rip open so I could step into last night when Hayden wasn't bleeding all over the floor, and I still believed I could save Noah, but I can't. I wish I was onstage, and Hayden was in the audience, and we were having a curtain call, and everybody was safe.

The ambulance arrives, and medics lift Hayden onto a stretcher. I follow the stretcher to the door, along with Mom and Dad. We go outside. Still no sign of Hayden's folks.

When the ambulance pulls out of the parking lot, for just a moment I see a bright light shine out the back window. I pray it's Hayden's guardian angel with him.

By now, the police have arrested Jason Bowen and gotten him out of here. Most of the audience and a lot of the kids in the show have left too. Sean walks with me as I go back inside the school to get my stuff.

We take a shortcut through the cafeteria, and I remember the art show. All our work is on display, and Sean stops in front of the pencil sketch I drew of Mr. Bowen leaning down and talking to Noah. Bus 25 is just pulling away from the curb in the background. Noah's Darth Maul book bag is slung over his shoulder.

"I remember that," Sean says.

"Yeah?"

"I mean, I didn't think anything weird about it then. But I remember it. I remember him waiting for the bus." Sean looks at me. "You weren't there, Gracie. How did you . . . ?"

"I just . . . can," I say.

And my brother, because he's the wonderful kid that he is, accepts that as enough of an explanation.

I'm still wearing my bloody costume dress, so when we get back to the drama room, I change into my jeans. As we leave, I stick my hand in my front pocket, and there's Ms. D's note, blood-covered, but decipherable. I read it, holding the note in one hand and Sean with the other—who is, by the way, just a tad taller than me all of a sudden. We walk slowly.

> *"Dear Grace, When you walked into the auditorium two months ago,*
> *you dazzled us all. I think Helen is just the beginning.*
> *Love, Ms. D."*

"Nice," I say.

"True," my brother says.

Chapter 26

All us kids are stuffed into Peter's Buick, except Sean who's sick. We're on our way home from the mall. We had off today for Martin Luther King's birthday.

Mr. Jason Bowen was arrested two months ago, on closing night of *The Miracle Worker*. He wasn't arrested that night for the abduction and murder of Noah Dunne. That happened later. But he did get arrested for kidnapping Sean and for trying to kill me. And for shooting Hayden. It turns out he killed Noah the night he took him. The glimpse I got the next morning—that was Noah's spirit. I don't think anymore that Noah was hanging around because God forgot about him. I think he was just being the same ornery kid who took up for me in elementary school. He knew the boy Mr. Bowen had in that Thurmont house shouldn't have been there—and then, he had to save Sean.

The craziest kicker to the whole story is the boy. He's sixteen. His real name is Keith Matthias, and he disappeared from a small town about a half hour from here, Millers Station, when he was seven years old. He disappeared on September 11th, 2001. He'd been living in the house in Thurmont as Mr. Bowen's son for ten years.

That night, before Mr. Bowen got arrested at the show, the police found Keith on the road coming down the mountain from Cunningham Falls. At first, he couldn't tell them who he was. He just kept talking about not wanting *it* to happen to somebody else. But one question led to another, and eventually they realized Keith wasn't really Mr. Bowen's son. My family talks a lot about why Mr. Bowen never killed Keith in all that time but killed Noah so fast. Whenever the subject comes up, Sean and I look at each other. I know I'm flooded with images of Sean and Noah—light-saber battling, being pirates looking for buried treasure in Noah's weeping willow tree, hunkered down in our basement with their action figures—and I don't know why God took him home when He did. But I know that when he was here, he had a

191

blast. And I imagine Noah showing up in Heaven the night he died and telling God that he wasn't ready for the pearly gates yet because he had to make sure somebody stopped this creeper before he hurt Sean or any other kid. He still had some head ramming to do with his trusty lunchbox.

Now Keith is home with his family. And Mr. Bowen is in jail. And yes, Noah is dead.

As regards all the other stuff that the priest, and my dad, and even Caleb thought about Mr. Bowen and his tragic past, it all did happen. Apparently his wife did say bad things about him. And then she took it all back. And when his own son was fifteen, he did commit suicide. Maybe that's what made Mr. Bowen snap and become a bad person. Maybe he kidnapped Keith so he could have a son again. I don't know about any of that. I just know he became a bad man, and I'm glad he's in jail so he can't hurt anyone else.

And a part of me feels really sorry for him. I realize, more than ever, that God never gives up on us. He loved Judas 'til the end. I feel like all Judas would've had to do at the end there was say he was sorry instead of hanging himself, and God would've been thrilled to get him back. So I pray for Jason Bowen. If God thought he was important enough to send all His warrior angels to battle for that man, and if God thought his soul could still be won, I'll keep praying for that too.

Our family went to Noah's funeral. It hurt to watch Noah's parents and Julie say goodbye to him, and to imagine how I'd feel if I was in their shoes. I watched Caleb there too. He was sitting in the front with the Dunnes—it turns out his mom is Julie's mom's sister. He impressed me there. Not because he's so cute and has shimmery green eyes, or because his voice is to die for, but because he sat there and wrapped his arm around his mom and kept it there, even when they stood up and walked out of the church. He was her rock. I could like a boy like that.

But I'll admit I'm a little confused these days regarding all that romance stuff. Because when I'm thinking about Caleb, and how nice and cute he is, sometimes my brain does a flip-flop, and I see Hayden for a second instead of Caleb. And he's not too bad-looking, either. He was in the hospital for a while, but he's home now. And I'm glad. The day I got on the bus, and Hayden was sitting there in his old seat, I felt pretty happy. Thankfully, I'm still in ninth grade, and I can have as many crushes as I want.

I've been running indoor track. So is Caleb. I'm okay at it. I'm not the fastest on the team, but I'm not a humiliation to the O'Shaunessy name, either. Dad is madly advising me on what I can do to improve my stride for spring track. So is Bridget.

But Ms. D picked *Les Miserables* for the spring musical. I've done my research on it now, and I want to audition for it.

"Gracie, I'm not trying to hurt your feelings," my sister Bridget says. "And you were really great as Helen Keller. But *Les Mis* doesn't have any silent characters, right? Can you even sing?"

"Yeah," I say. "And I don't stutter when I sing."

"You've got really stiff competition," Mary says.

Now, as we reach our neighborhood, the heater in the Buick is finally beginning to work. We're all bundled up, even though we're sitting practically on top of each other.

"Padawan, I hear a lot of those kids are incredible singers," says Peter, using a name for me I've never particularly appreciated.

"Do you even know the show?" asks Bridget.

"I saw it," Mary says. "Remember? When it was at the Kennedy Center. I went with that guy from Sykesville . . . Darren."

"Darien," Bridget says.

"Right. I should've held on to him. He really knew how to spend money."

Bridget pokes her head in front of Mary to make direct eye contact with me. All three of us are shoved together in the backseat. Shea is in the front seat with Peter, playing deejay. "Don't you like running track?" Bridget asks.

I nod and smile. "Yeah, but I *love* acting."

"You can't compete with these singers, Gracie. And you kind of look like you're ten. I'm not trying to be rude—just honest. I just can't think of a character you could play."

I look out the window. January is a time of hibernating in Maryland. No leaves or flowers—everything frozen and dark. It's only 5:00, and it's already nighttime.

We get out of the car. Everybody's talking about tomorrow's meet— who'll win, who'll place, which competitors are injured. Dad is on the

193

Internet when we walk in the door, yelling about things they're saying on runningmaryland.com.

"Would you rather be just some kind of . . . extra in the play, or run with us?" Bridget asks.

"Well, I feel like the more shows I'm in, the better I'll get. Just being in it would be fun." They're all looking at me now as we take off our coats and boots and make a mess of the kitchen floor. I add, "But I do have a part I want."

I take off my hood and my teddy bear hat that I had my hair stuffed up into. I shake my hair loose. One by one, everyone looks at me, and gives voice to various expressions of shock.

"You cut your hair!" Mary says.

I love it. I got it cut at a salon in the mall while everyone else went to the food court. My hair had gotten really long. Now it only goes about halfway down my neck. I think it makes me look perky, and French.

"Why'd you cut your hair, Gracie?" asks Dad as I step into the family room.

"Because I'm trying out for Gavroche tomorrow," I say.

"Who's that?" Mary says, confused.

"The little boy. He's the kid who's really brave on the barricade. I really like that part. I've been working on his song. I feel like I can get it." I laugh. "Being flat-chested will come in handy."

Sean walks down the stairs, folds his arms, and tilts his head, appraising me.

"I like it," he says.

My family looks at me, realizing something imperceptible has changed. I, Grace O'Shaunessy, am finding my voice. And it's funny, but the person who deserves the most credit is a girl who had her own voice taken away by some dumb disease when she was just a baby.

I excuse myself and run up to my room. I jump into my bed, turn on my Christmas lights, pop in my earbuds, and start singing.

"Good evening, dear inspector. Lovely evening, my dear."

I've been working on my cockney accent too.

***

It's evening on the meadow. A breeze lifts Clementine's gossamer skirt

as she dances with the boy. His blonde hair glistens in a setting sun more spectacular than any he'd witnessed in his earthly life. Clementine grabs his hands, and they twirl across the field of flowers. Noah tosses back his head and laughs, utterly delighted by the sights and sounds of this place and the euphoria assaulting every fiber of his spirit. She will guide him this evening to another path, a place further away from the humans and their struggles. Clementine worries that she botched things—that she didn't use her angelic intervention to save Noah's earthly life, or protect Keith or Sean—and she was never able to express herself to Grace. She tried, but so many times Clementine just confused the girl, or worse, scared her. She takes Noah's hand and walks up the hill, wishing she could've turned her kiss into a gift. Perhaps the King made a mistake when he entrusted Grace to her.

Sweet, sweet Clementine, whispers a voice on the wind. *I didn't make a mistake.*

The young angel falls to her knees. Noah waits for her.

"My Lord?" she says.

Before you kissed Grace, I kissed her first. And with that kiss, I planted my gift.

"What gift?" she asks.

My love.

She tosses her long white hair over her shoulder. "Love," the young angel repeats. When she and Noah reach the top of the hill, she takes one last look back. Noah runs ahead to a figure standing in the middle of a garden—a garden that's filled with every flower imaginable. And at the same moment Jesus and Noah see each other face to face, Clementine sees Grace, faintly. A tear escapes and wanders down Clementine's translucent cheek. It's not a tear of grief. More like pride, or . . . love. Grace earned her own wings this fall, and not because Clementine kissed her when she was a baby. She earned them by choosing to love enough to leap even before she knew she could fly.

Acknowledgments

I started *Grace* in a writing class taught by Elissa Weissman. Elissa inspired me and made me believe I could transform a single chapter into a novel. Then I became obsessed—basically spending the entire next year living and breathing my book. Thanks to my husband Jack and my children Hannah, Luke, and Sean for reading, listening, and tolerating. And thanks for cooking your own dinners while I busied myself hanging out all day with the O'Shaunessys! I love you all. Thanks to Darby McHugh and Anne Bontekoe for reading and critiquing. Thanks to all my student actors who inspired the character of Grace. I pulled a little from this one, a bit from that one—Grace on stage is a compilation of many of my favorite thespians, and I have so many. Thanks to First Sergeant James A. Hockett of the Westminster Barracks, with whom I had a terrific conversation in regards to how police would handle somebody like Grace, and thanks to my friends John Barry and Richard Hann for more helpful tips about crime and police. Thanks to my daughter Olivia, from whom I borrowed the word "eavespeeking", and my friend Bobbie Gooding, from whom I borrowed Grace's cloud of saints. While serving on a Kalos retreat on the holy grounds of the Bishop Claggett Retreat Center in Buckeystown, Maryland, I finally had an important breakthrough regarding the spiritual battle scene that happens in Bowen's basement, so thank you heavenly host for your presence there. Thanks to William Gibson for his brilliant play, *The Miracle Worker*, and thank you Helen Keller for being Grace's hero—and mine. Finally, thanks beyond measure to eLectio Publishing and Christopher Dixon for taking a chance on *amazing, Grace*. I am sure seers walk the planet Earth, and that angels enfold us.

Made in the USA
Charleston, SC
21 August 2015